DEAD LETTERS

Joan Lock

Severn House Large Print
London & New York

This first large print edition published in Great Britain 2003 by
SEVERN HOUSE LARGE PRINT BOOKS LTD of
9-15 High Street, Sutton, Surrey, SM1 1DF.
First world regular print edition published 2003 by
Severn House Publishers, London and New York.
This first large print edition published in the USA 2004 by
SEVERN HOUSE PUBLISHERS INC., of
595 Madison Avenue, New York, NY 10022.

British Library Cataloguing in Publication Data

Lock, Joan
    Dead letters. - Large print ed.
    1. Best, Ernest (Fictitious character) - Fiction
    2. Police - England - London - Fiction
    3. London (England) - Social conditions - 19th century - Fiction
    4. Detective and mystery stories
    5. Large type books
    I. Title
    823.9'14 [F]

    ISBN 0-7278-7325-3

Printed and bound in Great Britain by
MPG Books Ltd, Bodmin, Cornwall.

My thanks to the staff at the Islington Public Library, London Metropolitan Archives, the Guildhall Library, the Metropolitan Police Service Library and Museum, the Theatre Museum in Covent Garden, the Crystal Palace Museum, The British Library, but, most particularly, Haringey Archives. These are housed at the excellent Bruce Castle Museum in Tottenham and contain marvellous material on the locality and the Alexandra Palace, including daily programmes, some of which feature the extraordinary Police Fêtes which used to be held there.

Individuals to whom I am indebted are: Pains' Chairman, John Deeker, for his identification of the fireworks and descriptions of their dazzling effects; Peter Lane, Executive Librarian of the Magic Circle, for information regarding the magician, Dr Holden – although I confess to filling in a small gap with a little fictional magic of my own; Ted Crocombe for getting me online; and my husband, Bob, for editorial assistance.

To Eric and Audrey – ever loyal

One

Several people saw what happened. At least, said they did. Indeed, thought they had.

But, as commonly occurs at suddenly momentous moments, their attention was drawn by an alert which then caused them to witness the immediate aftermath – not the event itself.

In this case, the alert was the long and terrible scream which pierced through the music and happy laughter – and halted both.

Detective Inspector Ernest Best surveyed the scene and admitted that it was beguiling. The warm August sunshine glinted off the brass instruments and silver tunic buttons as bandsmen hurried towards their appointed places. Flower garlands were draped over the terrace railings and around the lamp posts. Pretty dairy maids caught the eyes of rugged soldiery come to demonstrate their fighting skills. Chalk lines were being drawn and hurdles erected down on the sports field below him, and circus hands glanced up gratefully at the clear sky as they busied themselves fastening back the flaps of the cheerful red circus tent.

No doubt about it, Best decided, the day was going to be a corker. The feeling of excitement and expectancy was growing.

He raised his eyes to the longer view, to the distant domes and spires of the City of London and well beyond. Could that even be the rival Crystal Palace he could glimpse in far away Sydenham?

He had been furious when told to report for duty that day at the Alexandra Palace.

'You can't mean it,' he'd exclaimed.

'Oh yes I can,' Detective Chief Inspector Cheadle had retorted belligerently, fixing Best with his implacably baleful stare. 'That's just what I *does* mean.'

'But what about the Chancel case?' Best had pleaded. 'It's near to breaking. If I leave it now...'

'You're going,' said Cheadle, 'whether you wants to or not. What's more, you're taking six of the others as well.'

'But the place will be swamped with police and the divisional detectives will be there,' Best insisted, pointing to that day's copy of *Police Orders.*

Cheadle stared at him stonily, refusing even to glance at the paragraph which required that two inspectors, five sergeants, fifty-seven constables (three mounted and four in plain clothes) be supplied by E, G, N and Y divisions to parade at the Alexandra Palace at ten thirty in the morning on the 19th August 1880.

'Why would they need seven of us from the Yard just to catch a few pickpockets? The place will be thick with off-duty coppers anyway.'

'Shut up, Best,' Cheadle commanded suddenly. 'If you'll just shut up I'll tell you why.'

He paused, took a deep breath, leaned forward and whispered conspiratorially, 'We've 'ad a warning.'

Oh God, it was worse than he had thought. The chief's mind was going. They shouldn't threaten to retire him like that.

The DCI slid a piece of blue writing paper across the desk. In large, loopy black writing it announced:

PEOPLE'S PALACE DISASTER – 19 AUGUST 1880! The Hensworth explosion will be as NOTHING compared with this tragedy! But you stupid bluebottles CAN'T STOP ME! Want a clue?:

You would know me if you saw me but DARKNESS WILL HIDE MY FACE. Ha Ha. Catch me if you can!!

Quicksilver

Best glanced up at Cheadle. 'You're taking this seriously?'

'Ain't got no choice, 'ave I?'

'But the Hensworth explosion wasn't deliberate, was it?'

'Weren't much left to show 'ow it happened, so everyone just supposed it was just another steam boiler accident.'

Best nodded. 'Well, they are commonplace.'

'Oh, "commonplace" are they?' Cheadle mocked. 'Anyways–' he emphasized his words with more sharp jabs at Quicksilver's note – 'he never says that he done the Hensworth, does 'e – just that he'll do something worse.'

Right again. No, his mind wasn't going. Sharp as a razor as always.

Cheadle took a deep breath and held up his huge left hand.

Best knew what was coming – the pictures.

'The way I sees it is, we got three possible pictures.' He pointed to his knobbly forefinger. 'Picture One: somebody wants to get back at the palace management – mebbe some 'ard feelings over the latest shenanigans.'

He held up his second finger. 'Picture Two: them Fenians 'ave got goin' again sooner than we expected – or they're just tryin' to confuse us.'

He extended his third finger. 'Picture

Three: there's some old lag that 'ates police an' want to see us runnin' about like 'eadless monkeys.'

Which we are going to do, Best thought with some irritation.

But it was true that the business doings at the palace were in flux – as usual. As usual, North London's answer to Crystal Palace was being handed on like a parcel bomb in a grown-up game of musical chairs.

'Could be some dodgy dealings goin' on,' said Cheadle, who had a poor view of human nature. 'As for the Fenians, well–' he shook his head – 'bit out of the way for them, ain't it?'

Cheadle sucked his teeth and twisted the ends of his once luxurious moustache. Stopped dyeing it, Best noticed. Mrs Cheadle's sensible influence, no doubt.

Best nodded. The Irish American Brotherhood had not caused the Yard trouble for some time, but they had information that a London bombing campaign was in the early planning stage. 'Doesn't seem their style,' Best agreed.

'My money's on an old lag who 'ates coppers.'

'An Irish old lag who hates the English and coppers?' suggested Best.

'Mebbe, mebbe,' grinned the Chief Inspector. 'One thing's sure, 'e ain't given us much time to prepare – tomorrow's the day.

An' let's face it, 'e couldn't pick a better place to get his revenge on coppers than at the Metropolitan and City Police Annual Fête, now could 'e?'

Two

There were several ways for those bent on pleasure to approach the Alexandra Palace, which was perched majestically on Muswell Hill in North London.

The quickest and pleasantest was in the manner chosen by Inspector Best – from the west, by rail – right up to the building itself on the Alexandra Palace branch line of the Great Northern Railway. He was on the first special excursion train to arrive just as the People's Palace opened at nine. There was much to be done.

Already the weather looked promising. A pleasant warmth was beginning to dispel the chill early-morning mists and the still-low sun glinted off the necklace of ornamental lakes to the north – diamonds peeping through wispy cotton wool.

Good news for the organizing committee who were anxious for funds for the orphanage's new wing. Last year's fête had been a dismal washout. The rain had been relentless. Bad news for the likes of Best needing to thwart Quicksilver's aims.

Good weather would bring an estimated 40,000 visitors and more, making the catching of him more difficult and his possible target larger.

Best glanced back at the steam train now noisily tooting and puffing its way back to collect its second load of passengers.

Just one example, he thought, of how to bring in an infernal device. One which could be tucked among the picnic hampers, sunshades, umbrellas and wraps, and delivered right into the very heart of the building.

Best contemplated the palace's internal map and sighed. He'd forgotten there were quite so many rooms and converging and interlocking passages and corridors – all which could provide endless hidey-holes and escape routes for Quicksilver. The man shouldn't boast that he was smarter than the police. He didn't need to be. It was an unfair contest.

Slicing right through the building from north to south was the well-named Great Central Hall. This concert hall, cum theatre, cum meeting place, was immense.

'Holds twelve thousand,' murmured Chief Inspector Billings when they went to have a look. He was the uniformed officer in over-all charge and was looking worried.

Best gazed up at the multicoloured early Renaissance arched ceiling and along to the gabled ends where brick mosaics garlanded huge rose windows. At the south end a magical rainbow glow was already lighting up the flagstones.

The north end was dominated by the spectacular Willis pipe organ, quite the largest, newest and most advanced pipe organ in the country.

'Powered by two massive, steam-driven bellows,' said Billings. 'They're down there in the basement.' He pointed to the spot at the foot of the organ.

Best groaned. Steam. And in just the place for Quicksilver to make maximum impact.

'The engineer says that these steam boiler accidents are caused by bad maintenance, not explosives. This steam boiler is kept tip-top.'

'Yes, but it could be tampered with, could it not?' retorted Best testily. That basement could provide the requisite 'darkness to hide his face', he thought to himself.

Above them, stagehands were already stringing high wires and lowering trapezes and a revolving globe.

'Performances begin at two thirty,' said Billings, reading Best's mind. 'An orchestral concert followed by the circus aerial items, then alternating concerts and indoor circus until eight thirty this evening.'

'There'll be police bands in here?'

Billings shook his greying head. 'No. They're all spread around the grounds.' He showed Best the Great Police Fête programme.

A Division would be leading off at one with waltzes, gavottes, marches and quadrilles on the terrace; the premier spot for the premier police band. Divisions S and E would take over from them until seven.

H and R Divisions were to present a brisk selection of waltzes, polkas and schottisches in the Banqueting Hall from two until seven, while T, V and L would provide suitably sylvan music in The Grove from one to seven. Two more were to keep the crowds jolly on the cricket ground during the afternoon. Ten divisonal police bands in all. A static resource too useful to waste.

'I think we should tell them,' Best said.

Billings raised his grizzled and wayward eyebrows.

'On pain of death if they pass it on.'

Billings nodded soberly. 'Very well.'

With wives and children among the throng that would be a tall order, they knew. They had already decided, in conference with a frantic management, that the customers and performers, even though many were police officers, should not be told in case there was a panic like at the Liverpool Coliseum eighteen months ago.

There had been a bit of a fracas in the theatre bar and, perhaps to break it up, someone had shouted 'Fire! Fire!' The whole audience in that 3,000-seat theatre had rushed for the door at once. Thirty-two had died and many more were horribly injured.

Another reason for not alerting all policemen present was that, in Best's experience, when too many became involved each imagined he wouldn't have to bother so much because the others would notice anything untoward. However, in this case, he reckoned more would be better.

Best and Billings continued their tour of inspection which included two theatres, a concert hall, billiard room, reading room, rest rooms, retiring rooms, an Italian garden, a palm court and an exhibition hall furnished with ebony and glass showcases containing examples of British artefacts.

The men looked at each other. Flying shards could cause some awful injuries. As might the glass and crockery in the bank of refreshment rooms along the north side of the building.

As Best and Billings nodded and smiled at friends and acquaintances a sense of uneasiness grew.

Maybe, thought Best, an attempt should

have been made to call off the fête after all, despite the opinion that it would be impossible at so short notice and that such a move would only make matters worse. Maybe when the posse of superintendents arrived to hand out prizes and show the flag, they would change the strategy.

The spectre of all these senior men appearing to take responsibility was less than comforting to Best, who knew that the same principle applied to them as to the junior ranks – but even more so. More chiefs meant more pandemonium, less coherence.

Orders would be issued by one, countermanded by another, the men would become confused ... He'd seen it all before at ceremonial events and riots. Some chiefs would jockey for supremacy, others to avoid overall responsibility. There'd be more of the latter in a case like this, he suspected.

'What ho? What roguishness is afoot here!' Best instantly recognized the cheerful voice and turned to see the ebullient Detective Inspector Littlechild decked out in splendid blazer, boater and necktie: one of the extra men he had been allotted.

'Was coming anyway of course – to make my bow before the footlights – but I received a telegraph last night instructing me to arrive earlier.' He rubbed his hands together. 'What mysteries must we unravel here?'

Best explained. He was relieved to see the man. He might have a sometimes embarrassing relish for adventure and excitement but he was also keen and a hard worker.

'Cheadle not coming?'

'Not till later. Thinks an early arrival might start people wondering – same with the superintendents.'

'Bothered about panic?'

Best nodded. 'So, anyway, it's all low-key.'

'Right,' said Littlechild, his eyes glistening. He was a handsome man around 5' ft 9", and in his early thirties but looked younger. Indeed, it was his boyish looks which had helped him get into the branch in the first place. They were a good cover. No one believed the young joker was a police officer. Best didn't sometimes.

Littlechild's moustaches and whiskers were now full and dark and he delighted in combing them into different styles for different characters from his favourite disguises: lugubrious for clergyman, close and smarmed down for a butcher and rather wild for a soapbox orator.

'Keep a look out for any old lags who could have a grievance,' Best warned. Littlechild, a very active officer, knew more of them than most.

'Right,' he said. 'And this darkness thing, what do you reckon to that?'

Best shrugged. 'Could be that he'll do his

deed in some dark corner, there's plenty of those. Or after dark – but there won't be much of that. Any other ideas?'

He shook his head. 'Sounds familiar though.' He knitted his bushy eyebrows in thought and pursed his lips dramatically. 'Might come to mind.' He grinned. 'One thing's certain. It's not Dickens, Thackeray or Bulwer-Lytton!'

It was no secret that Littlechild not only swore by these three authors but thought no man need read any other. Indeed, he claimed that Lytton's tales of derring-do had made him become a detective.

'How about fire?' put in Detective Sergeant 3rd class John George Smith who had just joined them.

Sometimes, thought Best, the lad had a tendency to state the obvious.

Fire had been the curse of the Alexandra Palace. Only two weeks after its opening in 1873 the place had burned down. The management, encouraged by the initial public response, had found heart and money to rebuild the gutted building. This time, four water towers and extra water storage tanks by the Great Hall were included in the plans.

'It's a possibility, of course,' nodded Best kindly. 'Anyway, we've got the palace brigade on standby.' He paused. 'I'm just off around the grounds. Shall I take Smith here,' he asked Littlechild, 'while you keep an eye out for the rest of our lot and a special watch on the comings and goings in the theatres and concert hall?'

Littlechild grinned and twirled his moustache like the evil Sir Jasper. 'Righto. I could think of harder tasks than keeping an eye out for Little Dolly Daydream and a few rogues and vagabonds.'

'Someone's happy, anyway,' said Smith as he and Best set off.

'Oh yes,' laughed Best, 'and at least he'll recognize which of the theatricals are the genuine article.'

Three

The customers were arriving. They looked like ants converging on a bowl of sugar, but grew bigger and more colourful as they climbed the southern and eastern slopes of the park, shedding their outer skins as they went. On the smaller of the species, white patches appeared which were gradually revealed to be wide, flounced collars, smocks and sailor suit trims.

Larger and faster black shapes overtook the ants. They in turn metamorphosed into ponies and traps and hansom cabs conveying the more well-breeched pleasure seekers and West End artistes who would perform in light comedies that afternoon and evening.

Lumbering along more sedately were heavily laden hay carts due to take part in the afternoon's pastoral procession. This year's theme was English Rustic.

It was half past eleven. The programme of events proper began at midday. Already a gaudy sprinkling of Morris dancers and fair milkmaids brightened the growing crowds by the maypole on the terrace.

In sober contrast, a detachment of soldiers from Chelsea Barracks scheduled to perform hand-to-hand combat and an assault-at-arms employing a fiendish array of swords, bayonets, quarterstaffs and Indian clubs. Such men, Best thought, might well come in handy in an emergency. Unless, of course, they counted Quicksilver within their ranks.

The view over London was amazing. Just below was Wood Green and to the right, Hornsey village, then it extended for miles and miles till in the far distance one could even see Shooters Hill, near Greenwich.

Slivers of silver here and there hinted at the serpentine route of the River Thames. Now and then above the river drifted grey-white wisps which then rolled away in tiny, talcum-powder puffs.

Suddenly, Best realized what they were – steam from the Thames steamboats. He turned away sharply.

The last thing he wanted on his mind were memories of the worst moments in his life when he was aboard the *Princess Alice* pleasure boat as she was rammed by the collier, the *Bywell Castle*. She'd sunk in a flash with horrific loss of life.

Beforehand, the passengers had been just like today's crowds – innocently enjoying themselves on a well-earned day out.

He lowered his gaze to the sports field in the centre of the palace racetrack where Chief Inspector Cutbush and his team were busy marking out the ground for putting the shot: the first of the police athletic contests scheduled for that afternoon. No need to worry too much about that area, Best thought.

These events would attract a great many spectators: proud families cheering on their menfolk and divisional colleagues urging on their favourites. But Cutbush had an eagle eye and was in the know about Quicksilver.

The detectives moved off again towards the huge Tudor Banqueting Hall squatting low down on the eastern slope facing Wood Green.

Now *this* was just the spot to cause maximum mayhem. All those families sitting down to their cold meats or veal and ham pie washed down with Allsops Pale Ale and ginger beer. But somehow Best couldn't imagine Quicksilver using this for his Domesday gesture. Not spectacular enough, too domestic.

Best's eyes were suddenly drawn to a short and stocky man stepping out ahead of them. There was something familiar about the back of his head and his jerky, stiff-legged gait. He nudged Smith and nodded at the man whose pace now appeared to be quickening as though he could sense he was under scrutiny.

'He's familiar,' Best hissed. 'Seen him at Pentonville, I think. Keep him in sight. You go left and I'll go right.'

The steepness of the slope hastened their step anyway so they now appeared to be almost running – an impression they would rather avoid.

Who was that man? Best wracked his brains. Not a policeman, certainly. Too short. But that low balding patch edged by a lower fringe of too-dark hair and the centrally placed mole was very familiar.

Maybe he had arrested him recently? Or seen him on his last duty visit to Pentonville to inspect the line-up of soon-to-be-released villains? Odd that the man should be wearing such a warm tweedy suit on such a day, but that also seemed familiar.

Smith was gaining on the man and as he

drew alongside he turned his head casually to the right. As he did so his face broke into a grin. He slowed down, fell back, and veered towards Best.

'It's Dr Roper, the divisional surgeon,' he laughed. 'The one the blokes call Stompy.'

'Oh, blimey. I am getting twitchy,' Best laughed, pausing to get his breath. 'Fit little bugger, isn't he?'

'Must take his own medicine.'

They stood for a while, watching the children enjoying themselves on the funfair rides and pestering their parents for penny-lick ice creams and coloured balloons.

'He's not got the flick of the wrist right,' said Smith nodding towards the Mister Hokey-Pokey ice-cream cart. Both men laughed. Smith had been obliged to master the flick when he posed as a penny-poke man in Islington on a baby farming case a couple of years ago.

A harassed father was trying to marshal his family to pose for the photographer while others began to queue up for their souvenir picture which would freeze the image of this day for all time.

Showing off to pretty girls in pale dresses were young swells with centrally-parted hair, high stiff collars, starched cuffs and gorgeous socks. Some carried straw boaters jauntily under their arms – quite the latest fashion.

The pace was hotting up and it all looked very jolly – and harmless, Best thought.

As he turned back to the fairground his eyes lit upon the gusts of steam belching from the chimney in the centre of the merry-go-round.

Riding on the carved and gilded horses below, laughing parents clutched giggling children as they swept up and down, up and down – such a new sensation; Three-Abreast Gallopers were a new invention.

They waved and shouted excitedly to their friends as they passed by again and again, but their voices were drowned by the roundabout's thumping traction engine.

Best went cold. Of course, *that* would be just the place that Quicksilver would choose. There, where the fun and noise and laughter rang loudest in the sunshine. There, for all to see...

He began running towards the merry-go-round, a puzzled Sergeant Smith at his heels.

People turned to look at them, surprised at first by the sudden movement then start-led by the urgency on their faces.

'It's *steam operated*,' panted Best. 'Why didn't I think of it before...'

It was then that a scream rent the air. Then another, and another. Soon there was pandemonium and panic as others joined them in their run.

Four

The gilding on the magnificent Three-Abreast Galloper glinted in the sun as the ride continued turning merrily to the jangling accompaniment of 'Polly Perkins of Paddington Green'.

But all eyes were riveted not on its splendid carved wooden horses with flaring nostrils, but on the rider on the centre row. She was hanging down over her gaily-painted horse's neck. As the creature dipped in the very latest fashion, her head smashed on to the wooden platform. When it rose again the bloodied result was jerked back for all to see. Small wonder people were screaming.

The woman's body was slipping further down, Best realized, as she disappeared from view once again, and was becoming entangled with the poles of the adjacent horses. People mounted on these horses were trying to climb off but were frightened to put their feet on the platform. They, too, were screaming and shouting.

One of the showmen by the booth on the far side, his back to the roundabout, began to look round, puzzled. Another, younger roustabout, wearing a jaunty red cap, was casually making his way around the far edge of the platform – the noise of the music drowning out the screams. His attention was finally captured by the onrushing gesticulating crowd headed by Best and Smith.

'Stop the ride! Stop the ride!' yelled Best, waving his arms at the startled young man and pointing to the other side of the ride. The lad looked about, confused, but began to work his way in the direction Best had pointed.

The body was now almost fully on the floor, held in place only by her right foot caught behind a pole.

'Now! Switch it off!' Best shouted as the grotesque show moved out of sight once more. He made a turning motion with his hand and at the same time shouted again, 'Switch off!' mouthing the words in an exaggerated manner. The boy finally grasped the message and nodded.

At last, the huge steam roundabout began to slow and the awful tableaux crept into view again as the ride came to a halt. The body of the woman was now slumped fully at an angle across the floor and was beginning to roll towards the platform edge.

Best jumped on board shouting, 'Keep people back!' to a tall young man in plain clothes whom he guessed was an off-duty policeman. He beckoned two colleagues. Between them they ushered off the distressed customers, then formed a circular barricade behind which Best and Smith could assess the situation.

Best turned the woman over and felt for her pulse. There was none. He put his face to her mouth but could feel no breath. Her skin was icy.

'I think she's dead,' he announced, glancing up at one of the young policemen. 'Get the hand ambulance from the police office and inform Chief Inspector Billings that we need more help here. But be discreet – we don't want panic.'

The climb back up the slope alongside the hand ambulance had caused something of a sensation despite the fact that Best had pulled up the hood to conceal the woman's face and bloody head, and instructed the policeman pushing the wheeled stretcher to adopt his best matter-of-fact expression. People began to run alongside, trying to look in. Onlookers pushed each other out of the way. One woman fell, another tripped over her. This was becoming dangerous.

'Go faster,' ordered Best.

The increasing pace made the crowd more excited and eager. Thankfully, more off-duty policemen saw what was happening and also began to run alongside, arms outstretched, forming a barrier which helped hold the curious at bay.

Nonetheless, thought Best, as he got his breath back in the police office, it had been an unedifying experience.

The dead woman was middle-aged verging on elderly. Her gown was of grey and cream striped cotton, cream-fringed and piped at the neckline, wrists and hem. It appeared well-made but, like her once chestnut hair, a little faded. At the waistline there was a tiny, empty, watch pocket.

Her tight bun had been loosened as her head bumped up and down on the platform. Strands of hair straggled across her face and some were caught and held in the congealing blood on her temple. Her pinky-grey summer straw hat resembled a squashed teacake – either by design or from the treatment it had received being hung from the side of her head with the aid of a tenacious hat pin. It gave her lifeless face an unseemingly rakish air.

Best removed it.

'Find that divisional surgeon, will you,' he said to Smith. 'Too late to do anything for her but I'd like him here just the same. See what he can tell me.'

Evans, the palace's young acting manager, stood to one side wringing his hands and looking even more aggrieved than when told earlier about Quicksilver.

'It'll be a heart attack,' he announced.

'I didn't realize you were a doctor,' murmured Best.

'No, of course I'm not,' said Evans huffily. 'Ah.'

A sensible older woman from the children's nursery was helping him to undo the buttons and underwear tapes so that they could inspect the body for any other obvious signs of injury. They found none.

Best undid the tapes which supported the inner pocket of the dress, placed it on a polished mahogany sidetable and tipped out the contents.

They were sparse: a one shilling all-inclusive Police Fête entry ticket, a penny programme, a plain white pocket handkerchief, two hair pins, a pair of steel-rimmed half-spectacles, a black comb, a packet of Morson's Pepsine capsules and a purse containing five pounds in notes and coins. Not poor, then.

'It's happened before,' Evans insisted sulkily, staring at the inert body with an accusatory expression.

'What's happened before?'

'These old people come here, forget their age and do all kinds of silly things they wouldn't do at home...'

'I thought that was the idea of the place,'

Best murmured half to himself. His patience was wearing thin.

While he examined the items more closely, Felix, the office's jet black pet cat, leaped on to the table and knocked the purse and half its contents on to the ground. Best ground his teeth as they all scrabbled around retrieving them.

'It's a good job I'd taken note of these contents,' he exclaimed crossly and glared at Evans.

The man's distracting whingeing was becoming a hindrance.

'I believe you are needed outside,' he said to Evans eventually. 'Your calm demeanour will reassure everyone that, as you say, this is nothing unusual. And,' he added wickedly, 'it might prevent the press getting hold of the story and making it into something it's not.'

That made the acting manager sit up.

'Make a short announcement about a lady falling ill while on the roundabout – something to do with the heat,' Best suggested. 'But tell them that everything is all right now and she is being attended by a doctor.'

Evans dashed out of the room. His presence among the lingering crowd might well, Best guessed, make things worse rather than better, but at least it got him out of his hair.

They ought to have taken the body to the

police office as he had wanted to in the first place, but the only available space had been in a cell, and that was thought unsuitable.

Chief Inspector Billings put his head around the door. 'How are things?'

'No clue about her identity yet,' sighed Best who was keen to get back out to look for Quicksilver.

'Oh, dear, that's a nuisance.' He paused. 'Look, do you mind carrying on with this for a while? I've got an emergency over by the triple lakes.'

'Some idiot fallen in?'

'No, a pickpocket they think – or maybe just a bustle-bumper.'

Best shook his head. 'How they have the nerve with all these coppers around!'

'Bigger challenge, I suppose,' Billings shrugged. 'Anyway, they're not supposed to be able to stop themselves are they – with all these lovely ladies about?' He smiled dryly. 'We've closed the ride down and secured the scene. If you like, you can go back and have a look at it and bring the operators to my office for interview. We've taken the names and addresses from others on the roundabout – those we could trace anyway. I've told them to pop in here at around six this evening, just in case you need to speak to them.'

'Right.'

Best was torn. This wasn't quite what he

was there for, to deal with an everyday sudden death – or what certainly looked like an everyday sudden death. He was loath to agree with Evans but he was probably right. A heart attack after too much unaccustomed activity and excitement.

Then again it might be a suspicious death. Possibly even something to do with Quicksilver. In any case, he and Smith had been the first officers on the scene which, technically in one sense, made it theirs. But suspicious? He looked at the body again; no, certainly not.

'Oh, and I've telegraphed Wood Green and told them to get a hearse up here – but to make it discreet.'

Best wondered how they were going to manage that apart from garlanding it with daisies, mounting jolly haymakers on the roof and pretending it was part of the rustic procession.

'I think,' said Best decisively, 'that Sergeant Smith can handle this small matter while I continue the hunt for Quicksilver.'

Five

Joe and Jack Hare looked out of place even in such a simple indoor venue as a police office.

Father and son were both strong, square-shaped men with short legs, barrel chests, red-gold crinkly hair and fair skin burnished by their outdoor life.

They sat uncomfortably before the plain desk overlooked by a filing cabinet and a dour portrait of Queen Victoria, Empress of India.

The older man's chest rattled noisily as he breathed. The constant fresh air seemed to have done little to alleviate his asthma. Neither, Smith assumed, had the anxiety caused by the recent drama on their fairground ride. He must be wanting to get back to his roundabout to recoup some of the money paid out for such an expensive new machine, not to mention worried about his Alexandra Palace concession.

Despite feeling he should have kept a better eye on his customers, Smith took pity on the man, interviewing him first and in a

36

conciliatory manner. No need to rub it in. Anyway, you got nothing out of people by doing that.

'What can you tell me about this lady customer, Mr Hare?' he began.

Joe Hare shifted uneasily in his seat, took a deep and noisy breath and said, 'Er, nowt much, to be 'onest.

'You don't remember seeing her get on?'

'Er...' His eyes looked hunted as he sought about for words, then he pleaded, 'There's so many y'see and they comes and goes...'

'So you don't remember her at all?'

He shook his head, sighed and admitted, 'Na. To be honest, I doesn't.'

That was a blow for Smith but he could understand the difficulty. A familiar one for policemen in fact – trying to recall one person from the many who came into their orbit. Joe Hare saw his customers only for a moment, and there were so many of them coming and going. Why should one middle-aged lady stand out?

The man's anxious eyes reminded him of his father's, always at a little bit of a loss with the world.

'Don't worry–' he patted Joe's freckled fist – 'as you say, there are so many. You might remember something later.' Mr Hare's breathing slowed a little. 'Just let us know if you do.'

He nodded wordlessly but was clearly

unconvinced that such a thing was possible. If he didn't remember now – right after the event – how could he remember at all?

Smith knew different. He knew that at a time of shock your mind could be wiped clean of certain memories which later popped up in vivid little pictures. He knew Best got them – of people drowning, reaching out to him and screaming ... him pushing them away...

Jack Hare's manner proved quite different from that of his father and tediously familiar to a policeman with any service. Not exactly belligerent but hovering – waiting for an opportunity to let fly. Smith didn't give it to him. He treated Jack Hare with impeccable courtesy – a stance which clearly confused the young man – at first.

'Now I know this has all been very unpleasant for you both,' Smith assured him, 'and you have to get your ride started up again soon to make some money.'

Jack Hare sat forward in his chair and nodded vigorously. 'Yeh, we do.'

'Well, I'll be as quick as I can with this,' Smith assured him. 'But you do understand that we need your assistance.'

The lad opened his mouth uncertainly as if to speak but nothing came out. Clearly any previous contact with the constabulary had not been on these polite terms.

'You see,' Smith went on, 'we don't know

who this lady is so we need all the help we can get – anything you remember about her...'

'I don't remember nothing,' said Jack Hare abruptly.

'No, well maybe not straight away. I can understand that. But I'd like you to think back to what you were doing...'

'I have been – an' I still remember nothing.' There was a note of triumph in his voice. The lad was regaining his confidence and with it his ingrained hatred of the police.

He's also decided I'm soft, thought Smith. He looked at Jack silently for a moment then said, 'Well, if you do...'

'I won't,' he said.

'Ah,' said Smith thoughtfully, rubbing his chin, 'that's a pity.' The young man's expression had now grown insolent. 'You see, no identification does stretch the business out rather...'

'What d'you mean?' He sat forward bunching his powerful shoulders threateningly.

'Well,' said Smith icily, 'what I mean is, we will have to examine the place where she died much more thoroughly to see whether there was something there that may have caused her death. And the doctor will have to examine her more thoroughly – and he will have to come to see your machinery...'

He took a deep breath. 'Then we might have to get the safety people to examine it...'

The young man jumped to his feet, his fists bunched and arms drawn back in a fighting stance which doubtless served him well in the fairground. 'What d'you mean? There's nowt wrong with our ride!'

'Maybe so, Mr Hare,' said Smith coldly. 'But we're not to know that and we've got to be sure, you see. And, of course, the palace authorities will expect you to help us all you can, won't they now?'

There was a time for conciliatory tones and a time for making sure they knew who was boss, Best had always told him.

'I, well...' The lad was floundering now. Good. Smith put the boot in.

'You weren't keeping a proper eye out for your customers, were you? You could be closed down right now for that.' Smith paused while this message sank in. 'Now,' he ordered, 'please wait outside with your father until we are ready to continue.'

It was touch and go whether the man punched Smith or obeyed but the detective sergeant guessed that the mention of closing down and of his father swayed the matter and he merely glared and left the room.

Smith knew that many people lied to police on principal. Said they had seen things which they hadn't, but mostly denied seeing things which they had – even when

40

the matters were of no consequence to them. So he made sure that the pair were kept waiting long enough for their minds and memories to link up with self-interest and survival.

'My dad says he thinks he remembers something now,' a truculent Jack muttered as Smith emerged from the inner office into the waiting-cum-charge room where the two men sat side by side on a hard wooden bench.

'Oh, good,' Smith said, showing no surprise.

'Yeh. He says he thinks she talked funny.'

'Funny?' said Smith glancing at the older man. 'With an accent, d'you mean?'

'Yeh. That's right.'

'A foreign accent? French or Italian?'

The old boy shook his head. 'Nah. Northern or summat.'

'From Liverpool? Birmingham?'

'Dunno.' The man shook his head helplessly and held his hand to his chest before wheezing. 'Not London is all I know. Couldn't understand 'er at first.'

'How about Scottish?'

'Oh no. My wife was Scottish, I knows that.' He was pleased to be able to be definite about something. 'Weren't Welsh neither, cos the man on the swings is from Wales.'

'An 'e thinks someone was with 'er,'

41

exclaimed Jack.

His father frowned at him. 'I said I wasn't sure...'

'Don't worry,' said Smith. 'We know you could be mistaken.' And telling lies, he thought. This time claiming to have seen something you didn't, encouraged by your son who hoped this new co-operation would speed things up and who had realized that they would accept Dad's word before his.

'Was it a man or a woman?'

'Woman.' He frowned and waved his hand in the air as if trying to conjure up her image. 'Bout the same age as the dead lady, an' wearing a sort of grey dress...' He sat back and sighed apologetically. 'That's all I can remember.'

'That's fine,' Smith assured him with a cheerfulness he didn't feel. He wanted this all done so he could get back out with Best on the hunt for Quicksilver. 'Very helpful.' He stood up. 'We're a bit further forward. Right–' he slapped his hands together – 'let's go to see that ride.'

He ushered both men out of the office, thinking, Best is right. This job is all acting. That's all it is, acting.

They were stopped in their tracks by the arrival of Stompy, A Division's surgeon whom they had seen earlier and mistaken for an old lag.

'Right, where is she?' he demanded, smacking his hands together in a business-like manner.

Dr Roper was a quick little man with quick impatient movements who gave the impression of implacable self-confidence. Smith had no idea whether this was justified. Uniformed officers had more contact with divisional surgeons when they dealt with the results of mêlées and sudden deaths.

'No way of telling what she died of, really,' he said briskly giving her the once over, 'not without a post mortem.' He pulled up her eyelids. 'Hmm. Pupils a bit small.'

'What does that mean? Morphine?'

Roper shrugged. 'Could have been taking something with morphine in it...' He paused. 'How did she act when she died?'

'We don't know.'

He frowned. 'All these people about – someone must have seen her? Did she just slump, clutching her chest, cry out...?'

'We don't know,' Smith repeated. 'She was on one of those new three-abreast round-abouts, in the centre.'

'Wasn't there anyone with her?'

'No one we've found yet.'

'What about the other riders?'

'They all say they didn't see anything until people began screaming. To be honest, they don't get a very good view of each other –

they're too busy looking out at friends.' He paused. 'You wouldn't be able to hear any sound she made for the noise of the music.'

Roper grinned ruefully. 'So it's a good job I don't think there's anything suspicious about the death!'

Smith nodded uncertainly and cleared his throat. 'I was wondering,' he said.

'Yes?' said Roper briskly.

'The bleeding from her head?'

'Yes?' Roper glanced at his watch.

'Well, if she died from a heart attack why did she bleed afterwards when her head hit the ground? Shouldn't it have stopped?'

Roper nodded. 'Certainly very soon afterwards, Sergeant. But she might have been unconscious for several minutes before death. Hard to tell in this case, isn't it?'

Smith had to admit that it was.

When Smith finally got around to inspecting the roundabout there wasn't much to see apart from blood beneath the horse ridden by the unfortunate woman. He did, however, find scratch marks down the side of the withers where she had tried to save herself from falling – so she hadn't died instantly.

There was no lady's watch to be found anywhere. '*If* she had one with her it might 'ave dropped out of her pocket when she fell,' said Jack Hare, now making a show of being helpful. 'But we never saw none.'

'Pity, it might have had her name on it.'

'Tells us one thing though, don't it,' said Joe Hare knowingly.

'What's that?'

'Well, if she did have a watch, she weren't poor, was she?'

Six

When all the screaming first began Best imagined that Quicksilver's plan must be swinging into action. This was the disaster he'd planned for them.

Now, he knew that the death on the merry-go-round was merely an incidental diversion. Indeed, a normal occurrence at such an event only made more dramatic by where and how it had happened.

Quicksilver's puzzle still had to be solved and his presumed dire aims thwarted. Best cursed the time lost. He had not even completed his initial tour of inspection.

He resumed their patrol where it had left off, at the fairground. The swings were still swinging; small and shrieking bodies on straw mats continued to be catapulted from the bottom of the helter-skelter. Tiny tots clung on to red, white and blue balloons and kites. The ice-cream seller was doing an even more roaring trade and the photographer had his head tucked under his black drapes to immortalize a nervous young couple unused to being the focus of so much attention.

Some of the crowd were drifting south towards the racetrack to watch the haymaking and rustic procession while others headed north to the circus tent. Best joined the latter. He skirted the huge boating lake where perspiring fathers tried to make light of rowing around the central island in the heat, and indignant mallards and tufted ducks tried to avoid the persistent attentions of fascinated toddlers.

Who could Quicksilver be? Best wondered as he was being propelled down the slope by gravity. What person would be that angry at us? And why would they want to kill other people as well?

He shrugged. Probably something trivial. A copper clipped his ear when he was young or stopped him bowling his hoop – and it's niggled him ever since. He's probably just a nutter who thinks it's ruined his life. Ruin mine, too, Best thought, if he kills a lot of people.

Be more sensible to try to work out some of his riddles. That name, for a start – Quicksilver. Did it just mean he's too fast for us? We won't be able to catch him?

But it could mean more. He frowned and sucked at his pearly white teeth. Quicksilver – wasn't that the stuff they put on the backs of mirrors? Was this all to do with reflections? Was that it? Was he being philosophical – darkness ... mirrors...?

He arrived at the circus tent just as Shareef, the baby elephant, was making his triumphal entry. Perched on his head was a judge's wig of mighty proportions, while draped about his shoulders a judge's gown of similar unlikely size.

The alleged frightening appearance of Shareef was claimed to have startled a pony which had bolted, causing a lady passenger to be thrown out of a trap. She had fractured her collar bone and claimed damages for medical expenses.

Defence claimed that there was nothing frightening about docile little Shareef. To illustrate the point, his wily owners took him to the Royal Courts of Justice. An agreement was reached between parties. Shareef's time in court caused much hilarity and brought him much fame – which was being duly exploited.

This might be a good place to cause havoc – near this famous elephant which had been treated liberally by the law – where, possibly, Quicksilver hadn't?

As he entered the circus tent tunnel, Best

fished his warrant card from his waistcoat to show discreetly to the uniformed constable who was lounging by the entrance.

Instantly, the man straightened up, adopted a more alert pose and began to raise his arm.

'Relax – and don't salute me for heaven's sake,' Best hissed.

The constable, aware that he had been caught off guard looking less than alert, blushed and slowly brought his arm down to his side while glancing around surreptitiously to see if anyone had noticed. An act which succeeded in appearing far more suspicious than a full blown salute might have done.

Luckily, only the performers, scarlet-spangled bareback riders and diminutive clowns, were nearby and they were too engrossed in last minute adjustments to their costumes or chattering to each other in French to notice what some English policeman was doing.

Judging from the roars of laughter coming from the big top, Shareef's antics were going down well. The wild shouts of the children and the curious smell of damp grass under canvas evoked childhood memories for Best. He had sometimes helped his uncle Alfredo sell ice cream outside circus tents in exchange for a ticket to the performance.

Inside, the tent was throbbing with life. The audience, packed high and dense, was roaring its approval for Shareef and obeying instructions to shout 'Yes, your Worship!' and 'Not Guilty!', Shareef bowed in response, removed his wig with his trunk, doffed it, and bowed again. In prime position among the cheering crowd was a broad patch of deep blue and white – the police orphans – screaming their delight as hard as any.

It had occurred to Best that a circus would be a good place to hide away – with all the extra hands they take on for things like this. But Billings had not agreed.

'Not as easy as some think. They're a tight lot and these ones don't move about as much as most.'

'What about the clowns' make-up for disguise?'

'Oh, they'd notice that right off – it's all very specific. They all have their styles.'

'How about hanging about in the other parts of the ground?' Best recalled a clowns' cricket match at another police fête.

'Ah, yes. Now that's a possibility,' Billings had admitted. 'I'll tell the men to keep a look out for wandering clowns.'

Smith rejoined Best just as he was entering the Japanese Village below the palace's west entrance. It was a pretty sight with its delicate oriental temple and house together with the requisite stone lanterns and arched wooden bridge over an undulating stream, as seen on every Willow Pattern plate.

The palace authorities insisted that no trash would be sold in its bazaar but 'Japanese productions of the highest and rarest, as well as the most ordinary kinds'.

Judging by the orange and black paper parasols being carried aloft and handsome lacquered fans being waved about by obviously occidental ladies, their exhortations had proved reassuring. One or two little girls had even swapped their plain white smocks for colourful kimonos.

Smith's eye was suddenly caught by a woman's face in the crowd. He frowned. 'Isn't that...?'

'Who?' said Best. 'Where?'

'No.' He shook his head. 'I thought I recognized somebody – but it's not them.'

As they turned away Smith once again caught sight of the familiar face but said nothing. It was better like that, he was sure. Well, fairly sure. He wished he could ask Best's opinion, as he usually did, but in this case Best was the one person who could not be consulted.

The spaces under the stilts of the Japanese Village buildings made Best and Smith exchange wary glances. But they found no suspect parcel propped up against the wooden pilings.

Their movements, Best was pleased to see, had not escaped the notice of one very tall policeman. Fred Henley was an old colleague of Best's uniformed days on N division. He allowed his eyes to light upon the detective inspector for a moment, but had the sense not to offer any sign of recognition. Instead he shouted, 'Come on, out of there. Don't want you dropping matches and burning the place down, do we?'

'No, Officer, quite right,' said Best.

Rather than reassure him, the lack of sinister evidence made Best more tense and worried. 'Back to the palace for our meeting with the high and mighty,' he proclaimed looking at his watch. 'And, if we're lucky, a pint of ale.'

It was just as Smith and Best reached the top of the steps leading on to the palace terrace that Inspector Littlechild ran out of the west entrance.

Spying them, he shouted, 'Quick! Quick! Catch him!' pointing ahead to his left.

The mass of humanity shielded the object of his pursuit from their view. Nonetheless, Best and Smith joined in the chase, charging through the dense crowd as best they could.

The taller, younger and fitter Smith began

to outpace the two thirty-year-old inspectors but he glanced back to Littlechild for guidance as to just who was their quarry.

'Straw boater, cream ribbon, cream blazer,' Littlechild shouted breathlessly. 'It's him! It's him!'

They turned left on to the South Terrace but their man was still not discernible. On the grass below them, a dense circle of onlookers had gathered around an already inflated balloon. The surplus ballast bags had been removed and the ground crew were hanging on to the basket. But there was only one person on board, a man of late middle-age who was looking anxiously about him.

Suddenly, across the space between the crowd and the balloon darted a young man wearing a boater and a cream blazer. He flung himself at the balloon car and began to clamber aboard aided by the older man.

'Get him!' yelled Littlechild. 'Don't let him escape!'

Smith sped on like a bullet out of a gun, reaching the car at the moment that the middle-aged man pulled the rope undoing the neck of the balloon, and shouted, 'Let go!' Smith, too, flung himself at the wicker sides of the oblong car – and clung on as the basket parted company with the ground.

The crowd drew its collective breath and shouted warnings. The distance between earth and balloon was widening fast and Smith was still clinging on but beginning to topple backwards, his weight dragging the car and causing the balloon to wobble dramatically.

The pilot and the man in the straw boater realized what was happening and tried to pull Smith aboard. But his size and weight and the angle made it difficult.

The balloon was swaying alarmingly now and, still low, was drifting towards the palace. Was the fugitive trying to push Smith off? Best could not tell as that side of the basket swung in and out of view. At last the top of Smith's shoulders disappeared over the side – followed by the rest of his body.

A spray of sand ballast fell from the car as the pilot attempted to compensate for his additional, unexpected human weight.

The balloon gave a final, indignant shudder, then, climbing straight up, headed eastwards.

Seven

'What in God's name do you think you're doing!' The aeronaut's white beard quivered with indignation. 'You could have killed yourself and caused a terrible accident among the crowd!'

Smith pulled himself to his feet from his ignominious position in a heap on the floor of the wicker car. 'I am an officer of the Metropolitan Police,' he announced. 'And,' he went on uncertainly, pointing at the man wearing the boater, who was now incongruously holding a pencil and drawing pad, 'he is a fraudster!'

'Don't be ridiculous!' the pilot exclaimed as the startled young man's eyes widened in puzzlement. 'This is Mr Goodson, the artist. He is here at my invitation to draw the scenery from aloft. I am tired,' added the balloonist wearily, 'of inaccurate depictions of the views from a balloon drawn by persons who have obviously never even left ground.'

Smith was confused. 'But ... but...' He

glanced from one man to the other seeking help. 'He is wearing a boater,' he finished foolishly.

'If that's what you were after, sir, glance below where you will see such a person at the centre of some attention. What's your weight?' he added peremptorily. 'We'll never get to any decent height until we divest ourselves of your equivalent in ballast. Your presence was not allowed for on this flight.'

Smith felt an absolute fool. And angry that Best's impulsiveness had landed him in this situation.

'Sorry,' he said. 'Eleven stone six pounds.'

'Well, at least that's precise.' He leaned over the side and shouted, 'Beware ballast!' before tipping more sand overboard. 'Not something I usually do into the faces of my audience,' he scolded. 'It is as well that my reputation is already secure.'

'Sorry,' murmured Smith again who was now gazing at the man with awe. 'Are you Mr Coxwell?'

'I certainly am.'

'The famous aeronaut?'

'The same.'

'I feel such a fool.'

'So you ought.'

As the balloon resumed its upward flight, Coxwell looked at Smith's crestfallen face and said, 'Well, you're here now. You might as well enjoy it. Go on. Look over the side.

People pay me a great deal of money for this privilege.'

Littlechild marched towards Best, triumphant if a little dishevelled, firmly grasping the left wrist and shoulder of a young man. His captive wore a jaunty straw boater with a cream ribbon and a pristine cream blazer.

'Got him!' Littlechild exclaimed, grinning his enthusiastic boyish grin and awaiting applause.

Best groaned and covered his eyes. 'Tell me this is not happening, I don't believe this!'

Littlechild frowned. 'What's that, Ernest? What don't you believe?' He tightened his grip on the young man who, embarrassed by all the attention they were attracting, began to struggle peevishly.

'Here, hold him a minute, Ernest, while I get the cuffs out.'

He reached into his pocket and extracted a pair of the latest, lightweight US-style handcuffs. 'Where's young Smith?' he grinned. 'Couldn't he keep up?'

Best was tempted to release the prisoner to gesture upwards. Instead he jerked his head skywards exclaiming bitterly, 'He's up there!'

'Gone for a ride?' Littlechild chuckled as he snapped the cuffs around the man's wrists. 'Surprised you could spare him.' At last he registered Best's fraught glance – but misinterpreted it. 'Oh, I *see* – he's getting an overall view.' He lowered his voice conspiratorially: 'Trying to spot Quicksilver from above. Very smart.'

His prisoner now securely attached to him, he glanced up and watched the balloon drifting towards Tottenham. 'But,' he pursed his lips and shook his head knowingly, 'it isn't staying over the park for long, is it?' He looked thoughtful. 'And what if he does see something suspicious? How would he get the news back to you?' He chuckled. 'Haven't got a telegraph machine on board, have they?' He patted Best's arm. 'Maybe they have a carrier pigeon!'

The disbelief on Cheadle's face was matched by the scathing tone in his voice: 'Sergeant Smith is sailing away in a *balloon*!'

Best nodded apologetically. 'Yes.'

'My fault, I'm afraid,' exclaimed Littlechild gallantly. 'He and Inspector Best were helping me in my pursuit of Bermondsey Bill but the crowds were so thick and...'

'Who's 'e? This Bermondsey Bill?'

Littlechild cleared his throat. 'He's a long-firm swindler – built up all these phantom companies and...' Even the relentlessly ebullient Littlechild suddenly sensed a trap. 'Er – there's a warrant out for him, do you see.'

Cheadle contemplated them in silence for a moment, then took a deep breath and enquired in a voice heavy with irony, 'When you 'ad 'im, this Bermondsey Bill, did 'e by any chance have primed pipe bombs about his person?' Receiving no response, the Chief Inspector continued, 'No, don't tell me – I got it – you caught 'im red-handed planting a fiendish device?'

Littlechild looked down, shook his head and had the sense to remain silent. They all knew that once this mood was upon him the only thing to do was just stand there and take it.

Cheadle slammed his fist on the table. ' 'Ere's us, trying to stop somebody killing 'undreds of people – including our own – an' 'ere's *you* running about executing warrants and sending sergeants off on balloon rides!'

Another judiciously silent moment was eventually broken by Best who drew a breath and plunged in: 'To be fair, Chief Inspector,' he said, 'Bermondsey Bill *might* have been Quicksilver. Could in fact *be* Quicksilver and have already deposited his bomb – or bombs.'

More silence greeted his remark. This time, it was largely due to the depressing accuracy of the thought bearing in on them that, in fact, anyone could be Quicksilver – and their chances of catching him were minimal.

Cheadle broke the silence. 'Well, I just hope your men are keeping their eyes open, that's all I can say.'

Oh, they're my men now, are they, thought Best.

Cheadle sighed, felt about in the right-hand pocket of his commodious waistcoat and fished out a crumpled sheet of blue, lined writing paper, and said, 'We've 'ad another letter.'

He placed it on the desk between them, smoothed it out as best he could with his huge fist and passed it over.

The writing was wilder than before, Best noticed, and the number of capital letters and exclamation marks had grown – a sure sign of a loosening grip.

TAKE HEED!!!
'What I promised will transpire! You will CLOSE YOUR EYES IN ENDLESS NIGHT – as if bereaved of LIGHT!'
QUICKSILVER.

'Very poetical, isn't he,' muttered Cheadle, shifting about in his chair.

Best stared at the words. 'Wish I knew what he was getting at.'

' 'Ee's gettin' at wanting to blow us all to kingdom come. That's what 'e's gettin' at!'

'Yes, but I do think these might be clues

he wants us to puzzle over. First "Darkness will hide my face" and now this "endless night" stuff. Then there's his name, Quicksilver.'

'That mean's 'e's going to kill us,' said Cheadle bluntly. 'That last bit – endless night.'

Best nodded, then, treading carefully, said, 'Yes, that's part of it – but isn't he taunting us as well? Showing how clever he is – telling us part of something, but not enough. Does the first mean he's going to do his deed at night – or something more...?'

'Well, you'd better 'urry up and find out.'

'Littlechild thought the first quote seemed familiar and I have a feeling about the second one.'

'Lot of good, that is,' said the big man ungraciously. 'What we want is facts – not fancies an' feelin's.'

'Well, if we find it was from a poem, say, and we knew the rest of it – it might help. He's showing off and...'

'I realize that, Mr Clever Dick!' Cheadle exclaimed. 'But what you going to do about it? That's the thing. Besides chewing it over like this?'

There was a pause. Best began to speak but Cheadle waved him to be silent.

'I'll tell you what you're goin' to do. You're going to put your detective brains to work.

Where can you find out about this stuff?'

'In reference books and from artistic, educated people who might know such things,' said Best.

'An' where, in this building, can you find these books of yours?' He made it sound as if books were the sole property of the likes of Best and this was all the result of taking too much notice of them. He could be right.

'There are some reference books in the reading room.'

'An' where are these clever, artistic educated people?' He made it sound insulting.

'Some of the West End actors might know the poetry.'

'Right. Go on then. Get on with it. I'll organize your men – ' he waved his hand dismissively at the letter – 'you find out what all that stuff means.'

The reading room at the Alexandra Palace was tucked into the south-east corner of the building between the Great Hall and the Eastern Conservatory. With its handsome, heavy oak furniture and plentiful supply of the latest, leading London and provincial newspapers and magazines, it might have been a gentlemen's club in St James's – except there were ladies present.

Two of them sat at the writing desks to the left of the entrance – doubtless recording the delights of the Alexandra Palace for their friends. They could then post their letters in the conveniently situated boxes just inside the door.

To the right, two pairs of elderly gentlemen, probably season ticket holders, were fighting a chess war to the death and a couple of young men were engaged in a desultory game of draughts. Several more men were lolling in armchairs, reading newspapers.

The walls behind these writers and games players were lined with bookshelves. Best headed for the section marked Reference still unsure from which angle he should approach his task.

Ah, the *University Dictionary of Quotations*. That should be a helpful place to start. He had reached out his hand to grasp the book when something about the stillness of the mousey-brown head bent over the nearest writing desk grabbed his attention. His arm froze mid-action. Was it? Surely not? It couldn't be.

Then he realized that the woman wasn't writing after all. She was drawing. Every now and then, she lifted her head, gazed towards the far end of the room for a long moment, then she lowered it briefly to move her pencil, before looking up again and repeating the process.

It *was* her. Looking just a little older, frowning with that utter concentration that was still so familiar. She'd not seen him. What should he do? Stroll over and speak? Now was hardly a suitable moment for embarrassing reunions. He would turn his back, avert his face and retreat with the book to somewhere out of her view.

Too late. Her gaze had shifted to the place where he stood foolishly immobile, his arm up, his fingers still grasping the edges of the dictionary.

She looked startled, her eyes and mouth opening wide in surprise. 'Ernest!' she exclaimed warmly. 'Good heavens!'

She looked pleased.

He feigned equal surprise. Took her cue as to tone, and hoped she wouldn't notice that he was blushing. 'Helen! What a surprise!'

That was certainly true. He lowered his arm, smiled his best, flashing smile, strolled over to where she sat and held out his hand. She half rose, took it, and indicated the seat opposite.

'How *are* you!'

'Shush!' hissed one of the elderly chess players irritably. Helen put her hand to her mouth to hide her grin and met Best's amused gaze. She looked around, shrugged then pointed to the door which led into the Exhibition Hall. They crept out conspiratorially and collapsed in giggles among the works of art and manufactured goods displayed in the splendid ebony-framed glass cases.

Fortunately, apart from a family being lectured by their father on the merits of the distinguished statesmen depicted in Staffordshire pottery, there were few other viewers to be disturbed by their hilarity.

It had always been like that, he remembered. They shared the same dislike of pomposity and sense of the ridiculous, and sometimes behaved like children together when thus provoked. But neither had been laughing when they had parted eighteen months before.

'You look well, Ernest,' she said, looking up at him. He'd forgotten how small and dainty she was, but remembered how strong in spirit. That had been part of the problem.

'You, too.' She had never been a pretty woman but she was neat and quietly pleasing in a way which grew on one. She had always said that he had good looks enough for both of them and that people's eyes deserved a rest after looking at him. She had claimed that she served this purpose admirably. But, nonetheless, it had been he who had been the most overwhelmingly smitten. He knew some thought that this was because she was a class above him. But they were wrong.

'What are you doing here?'

'A series of drawings of the palace interiors for *The Graphic*.'

'Oh, marvellous!' He meant it. He really loved the illustrations in *The Graphic*. He glanced at the drawing pad under her arm. 'Can I see?'

'Yes...' She looked around for somewhere to put her work down but there was nowhere suitable. 'Over a cup of tea perhaps?'

He shook his head. 'I can't!' His distress surprised him – and her.

She patted his hand. 'Don't worry. It was ever thus.'

She was right, it had been. But she had been absent as well – and for longer than he. Much longer.

'Serious detective business in the reading room?' she teased.

'Yes! Believe it or not.' He sighed. 'Very serious. I've just *got* to find the source of these quotes.'

He showed her his notebook. 'From a poem by Christina Rossetti,' she said instantly. 'That first sentence anyway – misquoted a little.'

'Oh, wonderful!' he exclaimed with relief.

She smiled fondly at him.

'Can you remember it all?' He was like an eager schoolboy.

'Let me see, it's from *Up-hill*. Er, it goes:

"Does the road wind up-hill all the way?

Yes, to the very end.

Will the day's journey take the whole long day?

From morn to night, my friend."

She hesitated, closing her eyes and screwing up her face with concentration and muttering to herself. Then she stopped. 'Yes, yes, that's it.' She restarted:

' "From morn to night, my friend.

May not the darkness hide it from my face?

You cannot miss that inn.

Will there be beds for me and all who seek?

Yes, beds for all who come." '

He grimaced as he jotted it down. 'It's all a bit odd, isn't it? What does it mean, d'you think?'

'Well, I'm not sure. Something to do with life and death, I think.'

'Well, that's apt.'

'She is a melancholy lady – blighted in love.'

There was a moment's tense silence before Best asked, 'What about the other quotations? If that's what they are.'

Helen shook her head. 'That "endless

66

night" is vaguely familiar but...'

'Will you help me find the rest?'

She glanced up at the conservatory clock. 'Is this urgent? I have a feeling it is – but I have to meet someone in twenty minutes.'

'Extremely.' He lowered his voice. 'In fact it could be a matter of life or death – for a great many people.'

'Well then, he'll have to wait,' she said firmly and turned back towards the reading room.

She'd said 'he'. She was meeting a 'he'.

The shapeless 'rational dress' was gone, he noticed as they made their way back into the hushed room. Indeed the printed cotton dress made much of her neat little waist and was gay with rose buds. But it was much too obvious for her, he decided irrationally. Not subtle enough. She was obviously being influenced by someone who didn't know her well enough to understand her appeal.

Eight

Detective Sergeant Smith had never been higher than the dome of St Paul's Cathedral. He could scarcely believe he was now in a balloon with the ground retreating further below him by the second. It was incredible. Wonderful. Breathtaking.

The gaping crowd had quickly become a nest of ants watching their Queen Bee disappear from the hive. Ally Pally had become a child's toy castle and the Great Northern Express, puffing towards the Wood Green Tunnel, a train set model.

As the shouts of children and showmen faded, all was silence. To Smith's surprise he felt no sensation of movement as they headed over Wood Green's grand avenues, now unprepossessing rows of rooftops. Things certainly looked different from up here.

Soon, the panorama became a patchwork of fields and farms. A tiny cloud approached the balloon car. They rode alongside it for a moment, then through it, as the west wind blew them both along.

Smith's open mouth and saucer eyes caused Henry Coxwell to venture a smile. He began pointing out one or two landmarks: lying alongside Lordship Lane which snaked beneath them were Graingers and Broadwater Farms, just like scattered sets of toddlers' building blocks, and the red brick turret of Bruce Castle was set in its own little park like a garnet jewel in an emerald brooch.

'Tottenham, where I live,' explained Coxwell when figures in gardens below began waving to them. 'They're my neighbours.'

Seeing all this was amazing enough to Smith but also to be in the company of such a famous man was overwhelming. A man who had flown higher than any other in the world – ever – probably thirty thousand feet!

An unpleasant smell wafted down into the car. 'Gas blowing off as the sun expands the balloon,' Coxwell explained. 'I'm afraid coal gas is not the most aromatic of propellants,' he conceded as Smith held his nose. 'Can't afford hydrogen!'

A little smell was a small price to pay, thought Smith, for such an amazing experience.

They drifted noiselessly on above the marshes which bordered on the River Lea: a lush green carpet on which clusters of flies seemed to have gathered. Tiny white puffs of smoke came from these clusters followed by resonant cracking sounds.

'Newington Butts,' said Coxwell. 'The Hornsey riflemen getting in some useful practice.' He leaned over the side and released some more ballast. 'We've been keeping low,' he explained to Smith, who felt he could touch the heavens, 'for the sake of our artist. He wanted a closer look over the palace. But now we will rise a little.'

Oh, did he! thought Smith and dragged his eyes back to the huddled artist. He could after all be Quicksilver spying out the land. He didn't look so dapper now. The smart blazer was rumpled and the natty boater had been knocked sideways.

Seeing his interest, Coxwell explained, 'Mr Goodson and I are of the same opinion on the inaccuracy of the sketches from balloons which appear in books and periodicals. We wonder just where the artist was at the time.' He laughed. 'Perched on a mountain top? Or was he a winged messenger in space? We want the viewer to feel he is in the car with us. But, as you can see, with this ever-changing view, he has to be quick.'

Smith did begin to see that the young man's manner was not so much secretive as distracted and even hunted, but he felt bound to continue his quest.

'Can I have a look?' he said, picking up the pile of sketches.

Mr Goodson looked up, frowned, then nodded distractedly.

The sketch of the palace grounds seemed very vague and scribbly to the young sergeant.

'He's been up several times,' Coxwell pointed out, 'and does a little more each time – accumulating information for the final picture.'

Smith's eyes were caught by several crosses near the Alexandra Palace. One in particular, beside the circus tent, was extra large and accompanied by an exclamation mark.

'What does this—' he began.

Mr Coxwell steered him away whispering, 'He needs to concentrate.'

The air grew cooler as they rose. Golden rays of a dipping sun slanted out from beneath a stratus cloud and touched the mistiness which hung over the bow of green.

'Epping Forest,' said Coxwell.

Smith had once picnicked in the famous forest with his parents when his father was still alive. It looked so different from here.

They sat side by side now at the writing desk with the *Dictionary of Quotations* before them, opened at the index. Best, unsure where to begin, had allowed Helen to take the lead, tracing key words, starting with 'night'.

Her slim index finger ran down the page, then stopped. She looked up at him, her face bright with triumph, then lowered her eyes to the spot.

There it was, between 'city of night' and 'clothes of night and light': 'Closed his eyes in endless night.' Gray, 157:17. Best opened his mouth to show his pleasure but she put a finger to her lips and glanced around warningly. No wedding ring, he noticed.

When they located the relevant page, she pointed to the name heading the left hand column: 'Thomas Gray 1716–1771' before running a finger down to the verse which read:

Nor second he, that rode sublime
Upon the seraph-wings of ecstasy,
The secrets of th' abyss to spy.
He passed the flaming bounds of place and time:
The living throne, the sapphire-blaze,
Where angels tremble, while they gaze,
He saw; but blasted with excess of light,
Closed his eyes in endless night.

Best crossed his eyes and made a face.

Helen tried not to giggle as she traced back up to the title, *The Progress of Poesy*.

Best nodded, half understanding. That was the title of the poem but ... He opened his mouth again. She silenced him with a raised finger and whispered, 'Let's try for the other half of Quicksilver's sentence first – "bereaved of light".'

This time they had no luck. The long list under 'light' brought no success and 'bereaved' proved equally fruitless. Best frowned his puzzlement at her.

'They can't include *everything*,' she whispered. Instead of hushing her, the elderly chess player suddenly let out a great 'Hurrah!' and clapped his hands as he checkmated his companion.

'Oh, apparently, it's all right for them to make a noise!' Best exclaimed in a carrying voice.

Helen was thoughtful. 'Actually, the more I read it, the more familiar it becomes.' She tapped her forehead, willing the source to emerge.

'With me, too,' Best said. And it was – 'bereaved of light' was very familiar – at least he imagined it was. But that might only be because he kept staring at it with such intensity.

'Write the Thomas Gray quote down, then we'll discuss it outside.'

As Helen spoke he saw her eyes settle on his cuffs. She had brought the ingenious Fleur de Lys studs back from the Paris Exhibition as a present. He smiled, held them up and gave Helen a rueful grin. She patted his arm and smiled back.

Best and Helen sat side by side again, this time on the garden bench which circled beneath the central fountain of the Italian Garden.

He breathed in the fresh air and looked around appreciatively at the elegant formal flower beds and statuary. 'You know there were supposed to be gardens on both sides of the Great Hall. Another open space to help prevent any fire spreading so quickly next time.' He sighed. Fire could well be on Quicksilver's mind – given the palace's history in that respect. 'But the owners found they needed to make more money, so they enclosed it and let manufacturers exhibit there instead.'

'That's a pity.'

'What I find difficult to fathom,' he confessed, dragging himself back to the matter in hand, 'is whether the *whole poem* is meant to convey some clue. I mean, should we take notice of this "blasted with excess of light" which he doesn't actually quote but sounds as if it could mean an explosion – or should we just concentrate on the words he's given us?'

She was perplexed. 'Explosion?'

'You see, we've been working on the assumption that with all this reference to "darkness" that whatever disaster this man is threatening might be going to happen after dark.'

'What man? What disaster!'

Best hesitated. He should not have revealed so much. But he needed her help and time was short. He took a deep breath and told her everything. She looked at him aghast.

'But you must get all of these people away from here – right now!'

'No.'

'What do you mean *no*?'

'How?'

'Blow a whistle. Announce it through megaphones. Get policemen to approach people and tell them – anything!' she exclaimed passionately. 'You're putting their lives at risk.' Her voice rose. 'YOU MUST TELL THEM.'

People turned round and stared, startled by the passion in her voice, then looked away embarrassed at having overheard what they took to be a lovers' tiff.

'There would be a panic. Garbled messages and rumours would spread. Look what happened at Liverpool. People would begin to run, fall over, trample each other to death.'

'You don't *know* that that would happen!'

'And you don't know that it *wouldn't*,' he retorted. He was starting to remember why they parted. 'Anyway, the authorities have decided that there's more risk in telling than not. The threats may not even be genuine but, ever since Liverpool—' He spread his hands.

'But Liverpool was in a theatre – a confined space!'

'And so is much of this...' He waved his hands to encompass the garden and pointed to the narrow doorways which led into more enclosed spaces. 'And the crowds are getting thicker by the minute.'

She sat silent for a moment, then said, 'Do you get many such letters?'

He nodded. 'Quite a lot. Mostly from nutters.' He hesitated then added truthfully, 'But this one didn't show the usual signs at first, huge deranged writing, lots of exclamation marks although it is beginning to become a little manic.

'Another thing, they don't usually show an intention to harm other people. They're mainly just complaining that other people are trying to harm them.'

'Could it be political?'

'Easily, with all this trouble in Ireland at the moment. But the Fenians are usually more straightforward with their threats – if they make threats at all. They usually just do it.'

She stared at him for a long moment then said firmly, 'Right, then we must get to work fast.'

'Sunset is quite late at the moment, isn't it? What time would you say, about ten?'

'Yes. So what time are the final events?'

He took out his crumpled programme.

'A circus performance in the Great Hall at eight, then a promenade concert and fireworks by the triple lakes at nine, to be followed by an organ concert. But people do begin to start drifting away straight after the fireworks to catch the trains home.'

'So, a good place to catch a great many people herded together would be at the railway stations or the Wood Green or Muswell Hill exits.'

'Yes, I suppose so.'

'Or while watching the fireworks,' they both said together.

'We have thought about that, of course, and we're swamping the area around the lakes with police.'

They went back to their poetry but there was a sense of desperation in the air now.

'This one seems more sinister,' he said, pointing at the Thomas Gray couplet. ' "Blasted with excess of light, Closed his eyes in endless night." Sounds as if he is straightforwardly talking about an explosion and death.'

She nodded. 'That's certainly what it seems he wants you to think.' She sat back and sighed. 'I think it's going to be very difficult to find something more specific in these poems.' She tapped his notebook. 'Apart from the obvious ones we already have: darkness, blackness, death ... But something might strike us later, when we stop thinking so hard about it.'

'Which may be too late.'

'Yes.' She looked at her watch and stood up. 'I must go to my meeting.'

He was startled by her sudden defection. One minute the puzzle mattered terribly, the next it was dropped.

'Will he still be there?' he asked confusedly.

She looked him straight in the eye. 'Oh, yes.' She paused. 'But I promise I will keep wracking my brains and also see if I can track down those other two verses.'

'So will I.' He hesitated. 'How will you let me know whether you have been successful?'

'I'll leave a note in the police office.'

'Where will you be going – after your meeting?' He tried not to look too eager for her reply.

She held up her pad. 'To do more drawing.' She held up her index finger in a familiar gesture, her little face so serious. 'I'll give you my route.' She took out a slip of scrap drawing paper and scribbled on it.

'And if you need to reach me quickly?'

'I'll leave a note marked urgent in the police office.' She looked up at him and extended her hand. 'Just in case. Goodbye, Ernest. It's been good seeing you again.' They might have been passing acquaintances. She smiled and was gone.

A moment later she was back again. 'Just a thought,' she said. 'Well, two actually...'

'Yes?'

'I don't see why Quicksilver has to be a man. If anything women are more devious than men – they have to be. And, another thing, not many men read poetry written by a woman, and his first quote was.'

She was right. It didn't have to be a man.

'Secondly, have you looked around that Denayrouze Diving Platform? Seems to be a place full of disaster potential to me.'

She was gone again before he could insist that she keep away from crowds, confined spaces, suspicious people – and danger.

Nine

Best could see what Helen meant about the diving pavilion being a good place for a catastrophe, what with forty tons of water contained in a tank where divers descended to demonstrate 'submarine work' aided by the Denayrouze submarine lamp and speaking apparatus. But he couldn't quite see how disaster could be inflicted, apart from releasing all that water, which would be difficult given the way it seemed to be protected, or interfering with the divers' apparatus. Maybe the water could be drained out to leave them stranded?

He was still contemplating the possibilities when he felt a tapping on his right shoulder. Turning around he found Dr Roper standing very close behind him.

'Young man,' the doctor said without preamble. 'I've been having second thoughts.'

Best knitted his brow in puzzlement. 'What about?'

'About that woman. The dead woman!'

'Oh.'

Dr Roper grasped Best's right arm and

guided him firmly away from the crowd gathered around the diving tank, stopping only when they had reached a dip in the ground below the east terrace.

'Did you smell anything?' Roper asked.

Best wished the man wouldn't stand so close. It was disconcerting. 'Where? On the merry-go-round?'

'No, no. On the body. On the body.'

Best shook his head and shrugged. 'No.'

'Hmm.' The doctor sucked his teeth. 'Never mind, that's not conclusive, is it? Some can and some can't.'

Best could feel himself becoming irritated. A bad sign. When he became irritated he tended to act first and think later. A tendency he was still trying to control. 'Is there some problem, sir?' he enquired, scrunching his right hand into a ball.

'Well, there may be and there may not. Let's go back to the office.' He took Best's arm again and began pushing him along. 'We can discuss the matter on the way.'

Only with great difficulty in these crowds, thought Best as he was buffeted by two young men hurrying in the other direction. He shook himself free from Roper but the man was too preoccupied to notice.

'The body hasn't been removed yet, has it?'

'Not to my knowledge, sir. They won't have had the time.'

'Good. Good.' Roper clasped his hands together and waved them up and down, emphasizing his words. 'You see, the thing is, no matter how good a doctor you are, you can't keep everything in here.' He released his hands and tapped his forehead. 'Not all of the time.'

'No, sir.' Ah, that was what this was all about – a professional reputation at stake. 'But why? It was only a heart attack. Wasn't it?'

'It suddenly occurred to me,' panted Roper, 'she was quite pink, wasn't she?'

Best thought for a moment. 'Yes, I suppose she was.' Indeed, her good colour had at first made him doubt that she was dead, but the total lack of breathing and other signs of life had soon changed his mind.

They mounted the east terrace steps.

'Hmm. Pity is, we haven't any witnesses to the death.'

Best refrained from saying they might have tried harder to find some had they not had his heart attack diagnosis.

'We may have more on that soon,' Best said as they turned left towards the manager's office. That was a half-truth. 'What is it that's worrying you, sir?'

'Not sure. Not sure. Just a feeling. Pink can be a sign of several different things – coal gas poisoning for instance. But of course that doesn't apply here, does it?' he said dismissively as though it was Best who had foolishly suggested that idea.

'Er, no.'

He shook his head again. 'Well, maybe it's nothing.' They turned into the office vestibule. 'But you're sure you didn't smell anything?'

'No ... well...'

'What?'

Best looked thoughtful. 'Well, when I put my face to her mouth to see whether she was breathing there *was* a slightly sweet smell. I guessed she'd been sucking one of those cachous ... The smell was familiar...'

'Almonds?'

Best stopped with his hand on the office door and frowned, trying to recapture the odour. 'I think you're right – well, sort of...'

'Burnt almonds?'

'Yes.' It was Best's turn to look concerned. 'That's a symptom of poisoning, isn't it?'

'Quite. Cyanide poisoning. But not everyone is able to smell it ... Unfortunately, I am one of those people who can't.'

Best opened the door into the manager's office.

'Felix is dead,' announced Chief Inspector Billings.

If only Betsy could see this, thought Smith. How she'd love the air up here and the view for miles and miles. The endless blue sky now turning golden to the west with the rays of the setting sun. As for little George, his twelve-year-old stepson, he'd be beside himself when he heard about this.

The aeronaut suddenly glanced out to the east and declared, 'I don't like the look of that sky. Anyway, you must get back to your duties?' He regarded the young artist, Goodson, who had never stopped sketching manically so as to capture the ever-moving scene, as he said, 'It will soon be too dark for any more of that drawing. Time to land I think.'

He peered over the basket rim at a flat meadow below and announced, 'And here we have the perfect spot. Flat, empty and not too far from civilization.'

'Won't the farmer mind?' asked Smith as Coxwell tugged the cord, causing a ripping noise which made Smith and Goodson look upward fearfully.

He'd heard that some Essex farmers had become fed up with balloons that had drifted their way with the prevailing winds, landed on their fields, ruined crops and terrified livestock. Some had even posted up proclamations threatening trespassing aeronauts with dire penalties – and worse.

'No,' said Coxwell, keeping his eyes on the ground and hand on the valve cord as he spoke. 'We can't do much harm here – it's just grass. Anyway, our landings aren't so catastrophic these days – much less of that dangerous dragging for miles.'

Smith was glad to hear it.

'Especially when there's not too much wind, as at present.'

Suddenly the ground seemed much nearer, and the balloon was starting to deflate. Then, at about 500 feet, they paused and almost hung there for a moment.

'Bend your knees, hold the side of the car and *stay in it till I tell you to leave*,' Coxwell commanded as he gave a stronger tug on the valve cord. The ground was now racing towards them and the balloon shrinking rapidly when the aeronaut stretched up and yanked down a red toggle. A terrifying ripping sound echoed over the meadow which made Smith and the artist jump with fright.

'Stay put! Hang on!' shouted Coxwell as the balloon settled on the ground and slowly deflated around them, sagging over to one side.

'Stay where you are,' Coxwell commanded again, 'until all the gas is spent. We need your weight.'

As the car began tipping over slightly, the artist hung on to Smith's manly form.

Soon they were absolutely stationary. The grappling hooks were thrown out to hold them down and they stepped out into a meadow silent but for startled skylarks.

★ ★ ★

It transpired that Felix, the black cat, had been nosing about the darker corners of the office, as was his wont, when he had emerged staggering from under a desk. He was soon convulsing violently and expired very shortly afterwards. He now lay rigid as a board at their feet with traces of white powder around his mouth and whiskers.

'Those capsules he knocked on to the floor, we must have missed one when we picked them up.'

'And Felix found it?'

'It seems like.' Billings shook his head sadly. 'He was quite a pleasant cat. A bit wild and bad tempered sometimes, but a good mouser.' He frowned. 'It's funny, with all of the peculiar titbits people give him here, you'd have thought his stomach would be strong enough to withstand a dose of indigestion powder.'

'We think they may have contained cyanide,' Best announced bluntly.

Billings' grizzled eyebrows shot up. 'Good grief!'

Dr Roper was leaning over the body, sniffing at the mouth. 'No, I can smell nothing unusual.'

'Dr Roper had some second thoughts about the cause of death so we came back to re-examine the woman,' Best explained.

'I thought I smelled something like burnt almonds from her mouth – that's why Dr

Roper's sniffing at it. But, apparently, not everyone can detect it.'

'So we have a *murder* on our hands?' asked the Chief Inspector incredulously.

'Looks like it. Can't see how it could be accidental if the cyanide was in the capsules.'

'Suicide?' Billings suggested hopefully. Suicide would be a nuisance but not half as much as a murder.

Best shook his head. 'Can't see it. Possible – but there are lots of easier ways to kill yourself.' He paused deep in thought, 'Unless, of course...'

A firm rat-tat on the office door halted his flow. Outside was a short, skinny, middle-aged woman wearing a grey cotton dress and matching hat and breathing rather heavily. She had obviously been hurrying.

'Hello,' she panted, placing her fist on her chest and patting it as though to ease her breathing. 'Is this the right place? I'm Miss Maud Forrest – they said our Alice was here.'

Her accent was northern. The rising inflexion suggested Tyneside, or thereabouts, Best thought but he was no expert on such matters.

Best pulled the door to behind him. 'Alice?' He paused, then enquired, 'Is she your sister or...?'

'My maid – Alice Harper.' The woman

clasped her hand to her chest again. Best showed her to a chair. 'Sit down, and take your time.'

She glanced up at him anxiously. 'She's all right, isn't she? Someone said she'd taken badly when she was on that merry-go-round. Why she wanted to go on the thing I don't know!' She stopped and smiled indulgently. 'But she's not seen one as grand as that before.' She took a deep breath. 'I expect she fainted with the excitement of it all.' She dabbed at her reddened cheeks with a handkerchief. 'It's so hot, isn't it?'

At last she became aware of Best's silence and the seriousness of his expression.

'She *is* all right, is she not?' Her glance shot to the closed office door, then up at him, dread dawning in her eyes. She began struggling to her feet. 'She's not just my maid, she's my best friend and...'

Best restrained her gently. 'Tell me what Alice looks like and what she's wearing?' He didn't really have any doubt but it was better to be sure.

Maud whispered, 'Well, she's a little bit younger than me – about ten years – though she'd never say exactly. She's on the short side, just like me but she's plumper.' She touched her hair and patted it absently. 'Alice's hair is reddish – going a bit grey now though.'

She paused, uncertainly. Best nodded for

her to continue.

'She's wearing her grey and cream striped cotton dress today – the one with the fringes on the...'

She registered Best's increasingly compassionate expression.

'What's happened?' she cried out. 'Tell me what's happened!'

Best drew up a chair and sat down opposite her. 'Miss Forrest,' he said quietly, 'I'm very sorry to have to tell you that your friend Alice is dead.'

'Dead! What do you mean, man, dead?' Her voice had risen almost to a shout as she strove to make the unthinkable untrue by denying it. 'What're you talkin' about! She cannot be dead, man. She was fine, when I left her, waiting her turn on that roundabout. Right, fine! I only went for some ice cream...'

Best reached for her hand and held it tightly. 'She just collapsed.' He shook his head. 'We're not sure why – yet. It could have been a heart attack.' No point in complicating things by talk of poisoning at this stage. 'There was nothing anyone could do.'

'But there was nothing wrong with her heart! All she's ever had was a bit of indigestion and she was under the doctor for that...' Maud began to sob piteously. 'She's my friend,' she wailed. 'She's all I've got in the world!'

Grief affects people in different ways. After the initial shock some remain stunned and speechless, retreating into themselves. Others cry, sob and even scream and throw themselves about. Some became garrulous. Maud, Alice's mistress, was one of the latter. Information came pouring out of her in a ceaseless torrent. A gabbling flow.

It seemed that Maud and Alice had lived together at Wood Green, close to the eastern entrance to Alexandra Palace, but they had not been there long.

They both hailed from a village near Newcastle-upon-Tyne. Best had guessed the accent correctly.

'We came south for my chest,' Maud confided, bringing her right fist to her scrawny bosom again and banging it lightly up and down. 'Always been weak. An' it gets very cold up there in the winter. You wouldn't believe the wind that blows up that Tyne Valley. Comes straight down from the Arctic, you know.'

Ten

'This Maud woman – did she do it?' asked Cheadle in his blunt fashion. He was being brought up to date in the police office where he had insisted Best stay on the case.

Best was startled by the idea. 'Oh, no. The woman is distraught. Alice was all she had!'

'Hmph.' Cheadle gave him an old-fashioned look. 'That right?'

Well deserved, thought Best. I must be going soft in the head. He sat up straighter and became more businesslike.

'I know there doesn't seem to be anyone else in the picture so far,' he admitted. 'But it's early days yet.'

Cheadle gave the semblance of a rueful grin. 'If she did, it would be a right turnabout. It's usually the skivvies what do the dirty deed.'

He was right there. Down the years, since the early days of the Detective Branch, there had been a steady trickle of murders of employers by their servants. Indeed, it was the alleged bungled handling of one such famous case, the murder of Lord William

Russell by his valet, Courvoisier, which had been partly responsible for the founding of the department. Best suspected that it was a crime of which Cheadle didn't totally disapprove.

Recently there had been a veritable spate of servants arrested for murder or attempted murder, but police had found great difficulty in proving them.

Indeed, they were particularly difficult cases as the suspects usually had the advantage of plenty of time and opportunity to cover their tracks. Also, the accused tended to have a record for dishonesty so were practised at dissembling when confronted by the police. The murder of Madame Riel, eight years ago, had been an exception.

No problem in solving that, since her French cook had fled back to Paris just before the lady, who was mistress to Lord Lucan, the general who had ordered the Charge of the Light Brigade, was found battered to death.

Detectives tracked the cook down. She confessed and was sentenced to death. When evidence surfaced of her quixotic mistress's uncertain temper, she was reprieved and sentenced to life imprisonment.

Despite the passing of the new Master/ Servant Act of 1876, which was meant to improve their lot, several more servants had come under suspicion.

Housemaid Mary Donovan had been arrested in 1879 for the murder of Mrs Samuels in Bloomsbury. But the police failed to prove that the stains on her clothing were of Mrs Samuels' blood or, indeed, whether they were human blood at all since there was no test to define this, and Mary had subsequently been released.

Scarcely a month later, partial female remains were found in a box which was half-floating in the Thames off Barnes. These were eventually identified as those of Mrs Julia Thomas. Her servant, twenty-nine-year-old Katherine Webster, was charged with her murder, found guilty and hanged.

Shortly after that, in May 1879, the remains of Miss Matilda Hacker were found at a house in Euston Square and servant Hannah Dobbs was arrested. However, despite declaring grave suspicions about her, the jury found the case had not been proved. Juries disliked bringing verdicts which resulted in a death sentence, particularly when the accused was a female.

'It would be even harder to prove that a mistress had murdered her servant,' declared Cheadle. He grinned. 'But I bet plenty 'ave done.'

The idea seemed to please him.

'But what could be the motive in this case?' asked Best. 'It's understandable with the servant who gets fed up with being put upon or wants to grab the loot.'

'Insurance?'

Best nodded. 'Yes, that's a possibility. I intend to ask Maud whether Alice was insured.'

'Not yet,' advised Cheadle. 'She might scarper and we ain't got no forwarding address, 'ave we?'

'Even if she's not insured, I suppose the strain of living in each other's pockets might have led to murder.' Best didn't really think so. Despite his natural policeman's cynicism, Maud's grief seemed genuine to him.

Cheadle wrinkled his nose and twisted a strand of his greying whiskers. 'Mebbe. But them temper jobs is usually a bit more violent, ain't they? Sudden rage and all that.' He sucked his teeth. 'When you are all boiled up you doesn't sit about fiddling with capsules and filling 'em up with white powder.' He laughed. 'You'd spill too much.'

Best thought that maybe simmering hatred might make him do just that – fill up capsules with deadly white powder to poison Cheadle.

'What you do,' Cheadle explained, 'is 'it them with a hammer.' He paused. 'Lots of times.'

He took a deep breath, then offered Best another of his priceless nuggets of wisdom. 'No, I reckon we got to look elsewhere for this one. There's more going on here than

94

meets the eye – you'll see.'

Irritating though his pompous pronouncements tended to be, the man was so often right.

Anyway, whatever it was would have to wait until tomorrow. The search for Quicksilver must continue or many more than one person might die. But while he remained at the palace he might as well talk to the eyewitnesses of Alice's untimely death.

He had completed his rounds. Helen and Littlechild were working on the quotes – some distraction might refresh his thinking.

Not that any witnesses would be able to help much when it seemed the whole thing had not only been premeditated but prepared beforehand. All the murderer had to do was wait till Alice got an attack of indigestion and hope that she took one of the deadly capsules. The victim committed the deed herself in fact. Very clever.

He glanced over at Alice's body. Why did he get the feeling she was trying to tell him something? Something he was missing. He looked her over again and saw only the same middle-aged, short, plump woman quite nicely dressed in quality but worn clothes – very likely her mistress's cast-offs. Nothing unusual there. Perk of the job.

'I couldn't believe it! Just couldn't believe it!' exclaimed Mrs Tancred, the excitable little woman sitting opposite Best. He'd already had the beginnings of a headache from hunger, the heat and all the strain of Quicksilver. This drama queen wasn't helping any. His head began thumping out its objections.

On the face of it, there had seemed little point in interviewing those who had been present when Alice died, when all the pertinent actions appeared to have taken place beforehand.

But bitter experience had taught the detectives that all was not always what it appeared to be. Hadn't Best once treated a sudden death as the suicide it seemed to be and allowed the witness who had found the body to depart from the scene? Later, when the case had metamorphosed into a murder, the gentleman witness in question was nowhere to be found.

In Alice's death, they had, as yet, no concrete proof that the capsules contained cyanide – merely a grave suspicion. After all, at the outset, the doctor had not thought anything was amiss. He'd only been gifted with afterthought. So Alice might have died of a heart attack, or had a stroke and indeed have been chewing a cachou beforehand – as Best had assumed at the time.

As for Felix, the cat may have partaken of some rat poison or the like. Easily come by in a place like this.

'I believe you were sitting on the horse to the inside of the unfortunate woman?'

'Yes. Mind you, I wasn't surprised she seemed to be falling off. Not a bit. Those animals are just too big.' She made them sound like living beasts. 'A little person like me can't get their legs around them.' She gave the handsome inspector a coy and girlish glance, incongruous from a thirty-five-year-old married woman. Girlish glances were a trait sometimes encouraged in very small women.

'I'm sure they must be, Mrs Tancred,' Best murmured, trying to keep the irritation from his voice. If he didn't get something to eat soon.... 'While you were struggling to keep on the mount, did you notice how Miss Harper looked – just before she fell?'

'Terrible! Just terrible!'

'In what way?'

'Her face was grey, ashen.'

Well, he knew that wasn't true.

'And she was clutching at her chest as if she couldn't breathe.'

'Did she cry out?'

He knew as soon as he said it that it was a silly question. They'd established that the noise level was too high to hear any cries for help.

'If she did, I couldn't hear her for the music – it was *so* loud,' Mrs Tancred complained. 'But she opened her mouth wide and contorted her face–' she opened her little mouth wide and grimaced grotesquely in imitation – 'as if she was screaming her head off.'

She was painting a graphic picture of a ghastly death. A sad thought. Aware of the effectiveness of her performance, her voice rose as she went on: 'Then she stretched her hand out towards me – like a drowning woman!' Her right hand clawed the air in mock desperation. 'But I could do nothing, nothing. It was terrible! Quite terrible!'

Well, he had asked.

'I'm sure it was, Mrs Tancred.'

'Then she fainted and fell forward–' she aped the falling – 'until her head hit the platform.' The voice was rising again: 'And then it began banging up and down, up and down! Then...'

Best sensed the opportunity for hysterics looming which was more than he could take at the moment. Mrs Tancred had already agreed that she had not noticed Alice beforehand so was no help in saying whether anyone had been anywhere near her previously.

Best leaned forward and patted the air in a calming and quietening manner. 'I understand, it must have been dreadful for you.' Then in a more businesslike voice: 'Well, Mrs Tancred, you've been very helpful.' He stood up and waited for her to follow suit.

98

She did so slowly with a faint air of grievance.

'We have your address and if we need any more assistance we'll be in touch.'

He began walking forward holding out his arms in a shepherding manner.

'Well, if you're sure...'

'I am. You've been very helpful.' Please go away you silly woman, he moaned to himself, and let me get a sandwich and a nice cup of tea.

Eleven

'A message for you,' announced Chief Inspector Billings as Best, somewhat restored by a cold beef sandwich garnished with creamed horseradish, put his head around the police office door. 'You're to meet Miss Franks in the Londesborough Room.'

'When?'

'Now. Straight away. She's just been in.'

He glanced quizzically at Best who knew exactly what the man was thinking: isn't she a bit out of your class?

The Londesborough Room? That was a strange place to meet at this time. Just as he was about to make some more enquiries regarding Alice's death down at the fair-ground – not to mention resume his pursuit of Quicksilver. He shrugged. Helen was a sensible woman. She wouldn't take up his valuable time unless she had something important to tell him. Well, he hoped she wouldn't.

At least the dreaded 'darkness', when they guessed Quicksilver would be most likely to strike, was not yet nigh, he thought as he strode through the cheerfully sunwashed conservatory, where the sharply pungent smell of damp earth mixed with the sweeter aroma of plants, flowers and palm trees.

The Londesborough Room, which housed medieval weapons and armour donated by the baron who gave the collection its name, was tucked just inside the palace's western entrance.

Clearly he wasn't the only person headed in that direction. The doorway into the ornate room was crammed; weary parents, eager for a chance to sit down, were shepherding in their hot, fractious children anxious to have them diverted for a while.

'Next performance half past six' said the notice on the door. It was now twenty-three minutes past. Performance of what? he wondered.

Another placard answered that question: 'DR HOLDEN'S MAGICAL ENTERTAINMENT'.

She imagined he had time for a magic show!

Chain-mailed and helmeted figures stood frozen guard on each side of the entrance and between the many glass cases which lined the room. Inside the cases glinted sinister medieval daggers, dirks and rapiers, plus pistols of every description. Many also glowed and glittered with inlaid and engraved ivory, pearl, coral and gemstones.

The walls behind the cases displayed even more ferocious implements hung about as they were with sabres, halbards, broadswords and shields. Were these what Helen wanted him to see? Did she imagine Quicksilver might seize some of them and cut a swathe through the crowds? It was possible, if he was deranged.

One thing was certain, this place was bursting with artefacts and people. It was just as well, thought Best, that Dr Holden was famous for transporting his illusionary equipment in a small carpet bag, in contrast to some of his rivals who required pantechnicons.

He could see no sign of Helen among the milling, noisy throng. Mothers were calling out, marshalling their stragglers, while fathers scraped and clattered gilt chairs to accommodate them.

This was ridiculous. Even if Helen were here, how on earth were they going to be able to talk in all this din?

Just then he spotted a small, upraised hand fluttering above the back row. He pushed his way towards her. When he arrived, she glanced up at him with a half smile and that direct, challenging gaze which had so startled him on their first meeting. No flirtatiousness or womanly anxiety to please here.

'Well done,' she said, lifting her drawing board from the seat beside her and patting the cushion for him to sit down. 'I was afraid you'd miss the performance.'

Performance! Here he was, handling a possible murder and trying to track down a homicidal maniac and the woman wanted him to sit down and watch a magic show!

She laughed out loud at his expression. 'You are so transparent, Ernest Best! How on earth you hoodwink criminals, I do not know.'

He couldn't help grinning back.

'Don't worry—' she waved a finger at him – 'this *is* important.'

He laughed. It was almost as if they had never parted. Here they were, instantly singing to the same tune again. He couldn't wait to tell her about Smith's balloon escapade. She would adore that. She had a soft spot for John George, ever since they had gone on a desperate search for him following the sinking of the *Princess Alice*.

He pulled himself up sharp, sternly remembering that he had found Helen to be a cold-hearted woman in some respects. Hadn't it been her fault that Joseph had died?

If she noticed the abrupt change in his demeanour she gave no sign.

'Two things,' she said as he settled down beside her. She held up her programme and pointed to an item listed as part of Dr Holden's performance. It read:

ALABAMAZER'S STYGIAN SURPRISE!
Far eclipsing the son of Thesis, as the performer Styx at nothing.

Best groaned at the pun.

'Stygian,' Helen insisted just as Dr Holden's slim, elegant figure emerged from behind a screen to take his introductory bow. 'Darkness, blackness, hell, all that...' She was still talking as the clapping ceased abruptly, leaving her lone voice ringing out.

'Shush!' demanded a man two rows forward. Dr Holden sent an icy glance in their direction.

'Besides,' she whispered, thrusting a crumpled piece of paper into Best's hand, 'I've remembered the other quotation.'

'You are privileged today, ladies and gentlemen,' said Dr Holden, twirling the ends of his luxuriant walrus moustache, 'to

103

witness exactly the same amazing tricks as those which recently enchanted Her Majesty at Balmoral. She was–' he smiled winningly at a woman in the front row – 'as near to me as you are yourself.'

While he was speaking, he had extracted a large, red silk handkerchief from his pocket, demonstrated that neither side of it concealed any object, then produced from it a huge bouquet of flowers, to the appreciative gasps of the audience.

'Her Majesty also loved that,' he flattered them.

There followed bowls of water containing goldfish and tumblers of wine to be changed into water, and water to be changed into wine. All the while the magician kept up his flow of distracting talk laced with humour and myriad puns.

Best didn't much care for sleight of hand, but he was fascinated by the magician's ability to distract on the one hand and perform on the other. Wasn't that just what Quicksilver was doing with them?

He turned his attention to the quotation. Best had always been surprised by Helen's unruly scribble; seemingly dashed off without a care and out of tune with such an artistic and neat person. He, supposedly the careless, volatile one, could produce copperplate immaculate enough to grace a testimonial for a retiring colleague.

From the scribble Best made out 'Blake' then:

And I am black, but O! my soul is white;
White as an angel is the English child:
But I am black as if bereaved of light.

He stared at the words while Dr Holden asked a member of the audience to select a card, then transferred its marks to a blank sheet of paper. An illusion which, he claimed, had even transfixed John Brown, the Queen's wily manservant.

All the time, diversion, distraction; getting their minds moving in one direction while he moved in another. A smoke screen. Like Quicksilver.

As they watched, Best became conscious of Helen's closeness. Her shoulder touching his. Even in this room full of sweaty bodies, including his own, he could detect her fresh citrusy scent. Always, he remembered, she looked and felt cool.

Theirs had been such a strange relationship. Begun in an icy, bristling atmosphere when she had stormed into the interview room at Scotland Yard demanding to know why he had done nothing to find her missing sister. A sister he hadn't even known was missing.

For a time, put off by her unbending manner, Best had even imagined that Helen might have done away with the pretty Matilda herself, out of jealousy and greed. He smiled at the thought now. The girl had surfaced eventually, in company with her fellow elopee and new husband, after nearly causing the death of Helen when she went looking for her.

While searching for Matilda together, they had grown close, this unlikely combination of quiet, mousy, independent, well-educated but struggling lady artist, and handsome, hasty, ebullient, half-Italian detective. But she had resisted marriage and kept him waiting.

Her reluctance was not due to the obvious differences in class and education but because she wanted to be an artist and was convinced that, for a woman, this aim was incompatible with marriage. When she'd finally said yes, he had been so distraught about the death of Joseph and her part in it, that he hadn't wanted her any more. Now, there was Mary Jane.

Mary Jane had not exploded into his life like Helen, but crept into his heart by stealth.

When he had first gone to lodge with her parents after the death of his wife Emma, Mary Jane had been a mere ten-year-old. He had seen her only as a lively and affectionate child whose impish smile had helped brighten his sad days and who soon began announcing to anyone who would listen that, when she grew up, she was going to marry the lodger, Uncle Ernest.

It became a family joke, but to everyone's surprise, even his, her dreams had become a reality after she had grown into a vivacious eighteen-year-old with a heap of black, curly hair and sparkling china-blue eyes. She'd caught him as he fell from the arms of Helen. No doubt about that.

He dragged his mind back to the moment and tried vainly to make something out of the words Helen had written on the paper, but they swam before his eyes. What on earth did it all mean?

Did they mean exactly what they said? Were they to look for a child – a black child? He hadn't seen any here – and very few in the whole of London, come to that. Maybe a child with a dirty face? No, impossible, there were too many of those.

Again, were they right to be putting all the words of all these poems together to try to make something out of them? Or should they merely be attempting only to decipher the phrases Quicksilver had used: 'Darkness will hide my face', 'Closed his eyes in endless night', and 'As if bereaved of light'.

Maybe tracking the sources down had not been such a good idea? It had complicated things and confused them even more.

He began digging in his pocket for his

notebook so as to cross-check nonetheless, when Helen tugged at his arm and nodded towards the performer and whispered, 'Stygian Surprise.'

The room went dark. A ghostly moaning came from near the entrance and began to move forward. As it reached the front, a skull was suddenly illuminated and it, too, began moving around the room – to the shrieks of some of the womenfolk. It was joined by a skeleton which went in the other direction as the moaning increased.

This was darkness and distraction! What might be going on under its guise? Murder even? A catastrophe? Best was tempted to demand that the curtains be drawn back and the light restored when, suddenly, it was – and the applause rang out again.

'Any good?' Helen enquired gently, obviously concerned by his increasingly anxious expression.

He shook his head. 'But something *is* coming back to me.' He stood up suddenly and exclaimed, 'I must speak to Littlechild.'

He began pushing his way along the row, forcing people to struggle to their feet and causing much heated response and hissing from those whose attention he was dragging from a Japanese conjuring trick 'never before been seen outside the Orient'.

His progress was abruptly halted by a middle-aged, bespectacled man who sat tight-lipped, refusing to rise and staring up at him defiantly. Instead of getting into a row about it, Best's hand flew to his mouth and he began retching, as though he was about to be sick.

The man shot to his feet announcing importantly, 'Clear the way! Can't you see, this fellow's ill,' as though it were others who had caused the bottleneck.

Of course, the theatre had to be at the opposite end of the palace. Best, now driven by urgency and a dreadful feeling of impending doom, was breathless by the time he reached backstage.

He could hear Littlechild out front, in full flow, his rich tenor voice wringing due pathos out of the ballad 'Angels called her home'.

Best reached the flies just as his colleague was returning to his seat at the centre of the troupe who were resting in a semi-circle with their banjos, trumpets, guitars and tambourines.

A rotund gentleman stepped forward and began a rumbustious rendition of the negro song 'Nancy Lee'.

The cheers and enthusiastic applause with which each act was received were as much an appreciation for the support the Metropolitan Police Minstrels gave the orphanage. Without them the place would probably shut down.

Best dragged out his now crumpled programme. Drat! The man who had now leaped forward was obviously Constable Haines performing his 'lively American Jig'.

They'd had their interval and Haine's dance was to be followed by a farce called 'The Haunted House'. How long would that take?

There was nothing for it – he would just have to attract Littlechild's attention. He began hissing and gesticulating. An angry stage manager appeared at his side.

'What do you think you're doing?'

'I must speak to Inspector Littlechild!' Best insisted. Unfortunately, his frustration made him appear a little wild of eye. The manager shot a glance towards a stage hand and nodded urgently at Best's anxious figure. The hand moved towards them but, at that moment, the company began their triumphal exit to the tune of 'Oh, Susanna'.

Now they were all around him, Best was unable to make out which of the shiny black faces belonged to Littlechild. Suddenly he was slapped on the back and the unmistakable voice exclaimed, 'Hello, old fellow. Come to shake a tambourine with us?'

Best was startled. It was hard to believe this woolly-haired, white-lipped vision was the scourge of the East End thieves.

Littlechild gave a gurgling laugh. He loved

disguise – particularly when it even confused his colleagues and friends. Once, he'd even turned up in it at his local pub after the landlord had bet him he would never be hoodwinked by his disguises – Littlechild had won.

'This is serious, John,' Best insisted, as they were jostled by the first of the actors to return to the stage.

Littlechild held his finger to his lips, pulling his obviously anxious colleague to one side. 'Go ahead,' he said, lowering his voice.

'That rhymester you arrested?' said Best.

Littlechild looked puzzled and shook his head. 'Rhymester?' What rhymester?'

'You know, years ago it must be. You told me about how he kept quoting poetry at you? I suddenly remembered...'

A roar of laughter drowned out Littlechild's reply. He waited a moment then repeated it, still shaking his head. 'Honestly, Ernest, I can't remember.'

He took out a large handkerchief and began dabbing gently at the perspiration on his face, taking care not to disturb his makeup. 'Years ago, you said?' He shrugged apologetically. 'There have been so many...'

It was true. A multitude must have passed through his hands.

'About five years, I'd say...'

Littlechild was keeping one anxious eye on stage. 'Ah.' He eased the rim of his boater to scratch under his woolly wig. 'Oh yes. Wait a minute. Something's coming back – vaguely. Very vaguely.'

His eyes wandered back to the stage and he leaned forward, listening intently to what the actors were saying. He turned his head quickly towards Best. 'This is important?'

'Very.'

'Look, I'm too distracted to think now – and I'm on.'

'I'll wait till the end,' Best whispered just as the Police Inspector 1st class launched himself forward with a whoop. It seemed he was obviously either meant to be a ghost, or someone who'd seen one, thought Best. Pity he hadn't seen this one.

Twelve

All eyes were riveted on the snugly-leotarded figure perched on the tiny platform way above them in the Central Hall. Robert Hanlon of The Hanlon Voltas was chalking the soles of his slippers. He carefully wiped his hands on a small towel, reached forward to catch the bar of his trapeze and tested the ropes.

There was a collective intake of breath as

the famous acrobat rose on his toes. The breath was held while he grasped the bar and launched himself out into the air. He swung back again to increase his momentum and out again. Then he let go, tucking his arms into his sides as he turned two mid-air somersaults before stretching out to reach for the opposite bar – just as it sailed towards him.

The audience let out a gasp of relief as his hands made contact, clung on, and he swung back to safety. Thunderous cheers and applause greeted his bow from the platform.

'He's amazing, isn't he?' said Littlechild as he appeared at Best's side. 'Sorry I've kept you waiting so long – lots of encores.'

The inspector was still wearing his burnt cork make-up and had obviously been hurrying. Rivulets of perspiration now streaked his features into a strange, caged effect. Best regretted his doubts about the man. He was an exceptionally keen officer.

'That's all right–' Best nodded towards the flying trapeze – 'but I don't think my nerves can stand much more of this.'

They wandered out into the picture gallery and headed in the direction of the police office.

'I've been thinking hard,' said Littlechild, 'and I've remembered this fellow. It was when I was on Division. He was a coiner, or was caught passing counterfeit coin, something like that.'

'And he spoke in literary quotations?'

'Yes. Now and then.' Littlechild nodded. 'He was quite an educated man, if I remember rightly. Swore that he was innocent, of course.'

'That's unusual.'

Littlechild smiled. 'Claimed he had no idea the money was duff. Made quite a fuss.'

'What did he look like?' Best rapped out.

Littlechild shrugged apologetically. 'Can't really remember, Ernest. Sorry.' He held up his forefinger. 'Just a minute. I *do* remember he had a bit of a lisp. He shouted that it was "mish-taken identity".'

Well, it wasn't much help, but Littlechild seemed quite pleased with himself, thought Best.

'Foreign accent?' Coiners often had.

'No.' Littlechild knitted his brow. 'At least I don't think so.' He paused. 'Sorry, it's not much help.'

Best sat down wearily on one of the gallery benches.

'Why are you taking all this on your shoulders, Ernest?' asked Littlechild. 'There's an army of police here – not just you. They're all on the alert.' He looked a little hurt as he reminded his colleague, 'And you know that keeping an eye open for Fenians has been handed over to me – so bombs and all that...' He spread his hands.

'I know, I know. I just have this unreasonable feeling that the answer is somewhere in here–' Best tapped his forehead – 'but I just can't get it out.'

'Well, nothing's happened so far, has it?' his ever-cheerful colleague comforted. 'I expect he just wants to see us all running around in a panic.'

'Something's going to happen when it gets dark,' Best insisted.

'Well, it certainly won't be dark down at the triple lakes. They're illuminating one of them with electricity tonight. Got to see that! Wish I'd heard the promenade concert – some splendid choral stuff.'

Chief Inspector Billings approached, his hand raised in greeting. 'Best! Been looking for you. That woman, Helen Franks, said to tell you she will be down in the pavilion by the triple lakes for the concert and fireworks.'

Answers were beginning to leap into Best's head: blasted with excess of light ... darkness...

Billings laughed when he looked at Littlechild. 'Another one! You chaps can't bear to take off your make-up, can you?'

'He was in a hurry to meet me,' explained Best.

'The one down by the lake wasn't!'

Littlechild was puzzled. 'What one down

by the lake? Couldn't have been one of ours, old fellow. We've only just finished our business.'

Best became very still. 'Is there,' he enquired carefully, 'more than one troupe of minstrels here?'

Littlechild shook his head. 'No.' The beginnings of a frown creased his brow. 'Just us.'

They glanced at each other. 'I am black but...'

'What exactly was he doing, this minstrel?' Best asked very quietly, his hands clenching into tight fists.

'Helping us.'

'Helping you? What d'you mean, helping you? Do what?'

'Search under the pavilion before the orchestra got into place.' Billings laughed uncertainly. 'It was funny. We lost him for a while down there – him being all black and...'

Best and Littlechild stared at him in disbelief, all expression and movement frozen.

'Well, we thought since he was one of ours...' Billings was floundering. 'Although I must say I was surprised that the fellow had a bit of a lisp – but I expect that disappears when he sings...'

Best was already up and running, shouting back at them, 'Run! Run! We've got to stop him! *We must stop him!*

Chief Inspector Billings was soon trailing behind Littlechild and Best. As the pair raced towards the rear doors of the palace they careered into a weary Sergeant Smith, just returned from his balloon fiasco.

He stumbled back, startled and confused, saw Best's urgent expression, noted the untypical lack of greeting and began to run with them. Soon, his long, loping stride was outstripping that of the maturer men. He glanced back for guidance, anxious not to make another mistake through acting too quickly.

'Pavilion! Triple lakes!' shouted Best breathlessly. 'Clear it! Clear it!'

The posse turned left under the gaily-lit railway arch, cannoning into several quietly strolling older couples escaping the noise and hurly-burly. They were enraged to be thrust roughly aside by these sweating, grunting ruffians, including a negro minstrel, make-up hideously smeared and wig and boater wildly askew.

'Disgraceful,' exclaimed a stout lady shaking her walking stick.

'The commissioner will hear about this!' shouted a wheezing, elderly gentleman. 'If I were ten years younger...!'

The speeding trio were deaf to their cries. The light music from The Grove behind them was fading, but that of the triple lakes orchestra was still muffled by distance.

117

Soon they turned right into the avenue leading to the lakes and saw just ahead to their left numerous gas lights twinkling as they were reflected on water.

'Not that lake,' shouted Best. 'The next one.'

The thump of the steam engine driving the electric lighting and the hearty strains of Benedict's 'Drinking Song' spurred the panting men to a final, agonizing effort. Best felt his lungs would burst. Helen was in that pavilion. Oh God!

The lake came into view and it was an astonishing sight. Suspended over it were two huge electric lamps. Myriad strings of coloured lights were strung out along the lake edges – all were reflected dazzlingly in the still, glassy water.

But the stunning lighting effects were wasted on the three running men. With horror, Best began to realize just why Quicksilver had chosen this site for his grand gesture.

The choir was in full voice, *'Drink, drink drink! And fill the night with mirth.*

Drink, drink, drink! Till we quite forget the earth.'

Oh, God help them. The pavilion was at the far end of the lake. They weren't going to be able to reach it before the song's crescendo which, Best was now convinced, would be accompanied by a terrifying explosion.

'Fill, fill, fill! Fill the deep-mouthed glasses high!

Fill, fill, fill! Let champagne glasses tremble.'

Please let it not happen, pleaded Best. I'll never lie again. I'll take confession again.

But it was no good. The music grew louder, the voices swelled. They were singing the final lines! The running men had reached the steps of the pavilion but could not hold back those final words. They rang out:

'Drink, and fill your throats with mirth,

Drink, and DROWN THE WORLD IN PLEASURE!!'

As the applause rippled around the waterside a speechless Best and Littlechild saw Smith trying to persuade the conductor to cease taking bows and to get off the stand. The man clearly thought he was mad.

Best reached the pavilion, sprang up the steps and unceremoniously pushed the indignant man from his podium. He jumped up there himself, faced the orchestra and singers and shouted between gulping breaths, 'Get off this structure immediately! Run! As far as you can! Run!'

The urgency in his voice suddenly penetrated their heads. Choir and musicians ran en masse towards the stairs, tumbling over each other, picking themselves up, then fanning out across the grass.

A startled, motionless Helen was sitting in a corner, pad on her lap and pencil raised. Best ran over, pulled her to her feet then dragged her, protesting, down the steps and away from the pavilion, stumbling and falling as they went.

'Are you *mad*, Ernest?' she shouted. 'Have you gone insane?'

'Well,' muttered Ringemere, the conductor, nastily ten minutes later. '*Very* impressive'.

'Well, nothing,' snapped a weary Best. 'Nobody said it was going to happen straight away. Anyway, nothing might happen. We may have nipped it in the bud.'

'Hmph,' the conductor snorted disdainfully. 'You realize that I have sprained my wrist and lost my baton. The leader of the strings has broken his violin and heaven knows what other instruments have been ruined. I presume Scotland Yard will pay for them?'

Best said nothing. He had already realized, as he sat disconsolate on the grass at the opposite end of the lake alongside the still confused and disorientated performers, that if, indeed, he had been wrong, Cheadle, and everyone from the commissioner down, would descend on him like snow in an avalanche. His job may even be forfeit.

It was always like that. Get it right and you were a hero, although rarely rewarded. Get it wrong and you were an incompetent fool, to be severely berated and punished.

'And just what are you telling them, our disappointed audience?' enquired Ringemere acidly as they watched policemen answering endless questions from the bewildered audience.

'That you heard creaking and felt movement beneath you and that we realized that the structure might be unsound.'

'How ridiculous!' Ringemere was furious. 'Blaming it on us! What a lie!'

'Of course it is a lie, you stupid man!' Best retorted. He could always run a pub. But would he be granted a licence now? 'We have to prevent panic,' he added wearily.

'Oh, and you're doing that, are you?' Ringemere nodded towards the puzzled throng milling back and forth around the three sides of the lake to which they were allowed access. 'They look to me as if they are becoming agitated.'

He was right. There was mounting tension in the air. A restlessness and agitation in people's movements as they gathered in groups and stared at the pavilion perplexedly.

Best turned to Ringemere. 'Well, do something about it. Show some spirit for goodness sake.'

'Me? What are you talking about, man?' Ringemere exploded. 'What can I possibly do to pull your rabbit out of your hat?'

'You can stop being so spineless and carry on playing and singing.'

There was a murmur of assent from those within earshot.

'Why not?' said a violinist, punctuating his words by pointing his bow.

'Yes, let's give it a try,' said another, nursing his rescued clarinet.

'You've got your voices and most of your instruments,' Best pointed out.

It was true. As they had run, the musicians who played portable instruments had automatically picked them up – as if they were their children whom they could not abandon.

'We have no percussion!' shouted Ringemere triumphantly.

'Well, I'll *find* you some,' retorted Best. 'Meanwhile, get yourselves organized.'

The musicians and singers began getting to their feet.

'I'll fetch you more players too – add a bit of volume,' he added over his shoulder as he left.

He and Smith made for The Grove where A Division's band were packing up after their performance. By the time they returned with percussion and a dozen musicians eager to add their volume to the Alexandra Palace Orchestra, the choir were lined up and ready to go.

As they swept into a jolly polka the crowd began to turn towards them with relieved smiles. Then a soothing cornet solo began echoing across the shining waters, switching the mood to one of dreamy melancholy.

That was more like it, thought Best. At least Ringemere knew how to use his music to capture and hold the spirit of the restless onlookers. The man actually offered him a half-smile of acknowledgement.

But Best knew that he was still in a great deal of trouble. Cheadle was stamping around the lakeside, peering into the crowds looking for him.

I can't face that yet, Best thought, as he retreated behind some of A Division's finest and largest.

He also saw Helen wandering about on a similar errand but did not reveal himself. Let them all go to hell.

This was not, he admitted, one of his better moments. He'd been certain that the eager, helpful minstrel must have been up to mischief.

A rich tenor solo was warning of the dangers of love with a passionate rendering of 'The Thorn'. Best's thorn was Cheadle and co. As for love? Well, it was too late to think about Helen now, wasn't it? Even if she had wanted him. He was engaged to Mary Jane.

As the ebb and flow of 'The Turkish

Patrol' began building into a rousing finale, a clutch of maroon shells shot across the sky, signalling the commencement of the fireworks display.

Organized by Mr James Pain, the show had been scheduled to begin at a quarter past nine and was not subject to a change of timing for anything other than torrential rain or similar Acts of God.

Suddenly, the whole lakeside and park was bathed in light from a multitude of star shells. Then a display of coloured rockets blended their various tints across the sky whilst two gas balloons, lit with magnesium flares and spilling sparkling fireworks, floated gently upwards.

On ground level, horizontal wheels began to turn, throwing off rockets, Roman candles and 'jewel mines' as they revolved. Fiery dragons raced, whistling, across a rope. They spun a few times, then rushed back again to the whooping delight of the now once more animated children.

And so it went on. Rockets, shells, Pain's prize asteroids and serpent-like saucissons whizzed about like whirligigs above them. Watchers scarcely caught their breath in time for their next gasps of awe.

The shimmering reflections in the lake gradually grew a little mistier from the drifting smoke. Suddenly all eyes were attracted to the coloured flares picking out the fire portrait of Colonel Fraser, Chief of the City Police.

Attention was drawn back aloft where a rush of multicoloured shells and stars and a golden cloud studded with jewel colours began the build-up to the grand finale.

Then it burst forth: balloons spouted tricoloured smoke, 'Aladdin's Jewelled Tree' flung forth its dazzling branches, and a wheel of multicoloured rockets sent out gigantic, cascading aerial bouquets. The sky was ablaze with light and colour.

Then, with a blinding white flash and a mighty roar, the Triple Lakes Pavilion exploded. Aftershock caused the ground to tremble, the audience held their deafened ears and the pavilion roof, fencing and remaining contents rained down all around.

For a few moments, as flames licked at the blackened stumps, the stunned crowd remained silent. Slowly, a ripple of applause began and built into a crescendo. People whooped and cheered excitedly in appreciation of this truly amazing finale.

This, surely, must be Mr Pain's most impressive firework display ever.

Best certainly thought so.

Thirteen

The dawn mists lingered over the damp and blackened stumps of what had been the Triple Lakes Pavilion. On the ground below these grotesque remnants, a line of policemen crept forward on their hands and knees through what had once been green grass but was fast becoming black sludge.

Two of the leading officers swept the ground before them with large magnets. Every now and then, they extracted small metal objects and fragments from the heads and placed them into bins alongside them.

At intervals, another officer came forward and emptied the bins into a large basket which he took back to a table at the rear. Here stood a stocky, tweedy, amiable-looking gentleman: Major Majendie, the Home Office explosives expert.

Best had become acquainted with the major at the time of the Regent's Park Explosion of 1874 when the man had riveted the jury with a dramatic demonstration of how and why the accident had taken place.

'What do you think?' Best asked as Majendie and his assistant separated out mangled music stands, instrument cases, lunch boxes and umbrellas that would no longer keep out the rain.

Majendie glanced up at Best, studied him for a moment, then muttered, 'I think you look terrible, Ernest.'

Best grinned ruefully. He felt terrible and, something he hated, rumpled and rather grubby.

When the mayhem which followed the Triple Lakes explosion had finally died down, he'd grabbed a couple of hours on a couch in the manager's office but been unable to sleep.

His mind had been in a turmoil. Elation and relief at having been proved right, mingling with his confusion over the lines of puzzling poetry and negro minstrels, visions of the carnage which could have occurred, and confusion at seeing Helen again. Despite a dawn wash and brush-up in the gentlemen's retiring room, he now felt seedy, exhausted and a little disorientated.

After all the extraneous material was removed from the table, Majendie was left with a much smaller pile of springs, wheels, cogs, nuts and bolts, a pocket knife, various mangled metal fragments and curiously untouched slabs of metal – some with nuts and bolts attached. A bent and twisted clock face completed the collection.

'I also think,' said Major Majendie slowly, 'that this clock was an exceptionally good timekeeper.'

Best nodded. 'Remarkable that the explosion came exactly at the end of the finale.'

'Yes, wasn't it.' Majendie inclined his head thoughtfully. 'Could just be a coincidence but these firework displays are usually well-timed and organized.'

'So, I'm looking for someone who helped with the display or who had been in a position to discover the timing?'

'Not too difficult?'

'No, I suppose not,' Best agreed ruefully. 'The starting time is published in the programme. They also tell us, and anyone else who needs to know, the approximate finishing time and...' He sighed. 'Just tell me – was it a professional job, d'you think? Have the Fenians begun their new campaign already?'

'Could be.' Majendie shrugged. 'But not necessarily.' He sucked in his lips causing the hair of his abundant silver moustache to fan out like silken wings. 'Needs knowledge to assemble these devices, of course, but, again, that's not so hard to acquire these days.' He chuckled. 'I can tell you that what you *do* need is a very sharp knife–' he held up the opened pocket knife – 'like this.'

'Two more questions: why do you have to

be so cheerful? And what was the knife for?'

Majendie patted Best's arm comfortingly. 'It was attached to the clock mechanism. At the appointed minute the knife dropped on a spring and cut through a piece of twine, which released another spring, which struck the percussion cap, which detonated the dynamite.'

Best shook his head dazedly. 'Amazing.' He paused, then enquired, 'So what I'm looking for is an incurable optimist with access to a knife grinder and a plentiful supply of dynamite?'

'Exactly,' murmured the major.

'A lot of flaming good that is!' exclaimed Cheadle, tapping his sturdy finger on a photograph of one Isaac Grimes, lately released on licence from Pentonville Prison after serving eight years of a ten-year sentence for coining and fraud. 'They all look alike!' he fumed, sweeping his hand across the album page. 'An' none of them will look like that now, will they? We keeps telling 'em but they won't listen.'

Grimes was the name which Littlechild had dragged out of his memory as his rhyming prisoner. 'They' were the prison authorities. The photographs had been taken in gaol just before the prisoners' release on licence.

In fact, things were beginning to improve

as the result of pressure from Howard Vincent, the director of the CID. But the changes had obviously not yet been significant enough to affect the photographs before them.

All these showed men wearing prison uniform rather than their own clothes which would at least have given them some semblance of individuality. They were not allowed to shave in prison so all the men wore feature-concealing beards.

For some reason, the opposite rule applied to head hair. This had to be close cropped. So, again, all heads looked similar. To add insult, the prints were of poor quality and fuzzy.

At least the hands, which were held up and crossed in front of their chests, tended to be altered little by prison life – apart from becoming coarser.

Hands were reckoned to be of great significance in identification. In reality, Best had found descriptions and pictures of them of little use unless they were badly scarred or minus a finger or two. Grimes, they noticed, had the full complement of digits and the backs of his slender hands were unmarked.

Cheadle, Best and Littlechild were gathered around a lectern in the Convict Office in Scotland Yard. All about them clerks and policemen strode back and forth, pulling down heavy albums from high shelves before poring over the pages of photographs of criminals under police supervision.

On the other side of a counter flap, released prisoners waited to report to police as their licences demanded.

'Be a waste of time circulating this,' complained Cheadle.

'Maybe *together* with this one,' suggested Best, pointing at the photograph of Grimes just after his arrest.

'The man won't be wearing 'is 'air and moustaches like that no more,' insisted Cheadle crossly. 'Would you, if you were 'im?'

Best had to admit that no, he wouldn't. In any case, the Grimes staring out from the final prison picture was so much thinner and hollow-eyed than in the post-arrest photograph.

'Be more confusing than an 'elp, letting that out.'

Best disagreed, but said nothing.

True, Grimes had been out for six months. Time enough, as Cheadle suggested, to grow a full set of whatever combination of facial hair he fancied, long hair with short hard whiskers and moustaches, or short head hair with exaggeratedly long and bushy side whiskers sweeping halfway around the chin. He might even be clean-shaven apart from a handlebar moustache and long sideburns. The choice was endless these days.

But surely those who knew Grimes well would still recognize him? Also Littlechild? The lisp, which had been duly noted, should also help him stand out.

'Look at that! Mother at Wood Green!'

'Well, I'm blowed,' said Littlechild excitedly. 'Right on the doorstep of the Ally Pally. Seems you might be right, Ernest.'

'Gotta be,' said Cheadle. 'Living nearby, has a lisp – and all that rhyming stuff.'

Best and Littlechild exchanged sidelong glances. 'All that rhyming stuff' would certainly amount to a flogging offence to the Chief Inspector.

'It's just,' murmured Littlechild doubtfully, 'it's just that he didn't seem the sort of fellow who would make bombs and leave them about to kill people.'

'Gracious me,' murmured Cheadle, with mock gentility. 'Yesterday we couldn't remember anything about the man, now he's being given a testimonial.'

Littlechild tilted his head in acknowledgement. 'No, but he's starting to come back now.'

'He certainly is!' Cheadle glanced from one to the other, the corners of his mouth lifting a little.

Oh, a joke.

Jokes were a recent departure for the chief inspector. Smith's mother at work again, they suspected. Cheadle was a lifelong bachelor when he met the widowed Mrs Smith, who had been asked to advise about the clothing on a body in the Regent's Park Explosion case. After they married, she had set to work chipping away at his crusty armour, sometimes with odd results – such as the jokes. The younger men laughed obligingly.

They went back to the chief superintendent's office, taking advantage of the added privacy and comfort while Williamson was on leave. Since Vincent's advent he had been moved alongside his men in this curious, two-storey block at the centre of Great Scotland Yard.

Chief Inspector Shore and Howard Vincent were over in Williamson's old office at this moment, preparing to report to the commissioner and the Home Secretary on the new bomber in their midst.

'I see our strategy worked,' Best said, pointing to a copy of *The Times* which sat on top of the pile of newspapers on the desk. 'I'm amazed.'

The press had given the usual generous coverage to the police fête, mentioning the circus, Dr Holden's magic show, the rustic jollity, the athletics, and the West End plays and concerts.

Indeed, *The Times* had declared, 'It would be difficult to crowd within ten hours a

greater variety of amusement than the programme disclosed.'

Mr James Pain's splendid firework display
had also been noted – but only in passing.
In fact, the only item which appeared to
have escaped the notice of the reporters was
the incredible exploding pavilion which had
marked the finale.

Had Vincent and the commissioner used
their influence on the press? Or had the
journalists swallowed the story that it had
merely been a spectacular addition to the
usual programme? The structure had proved unsound so the authorities had seized the
opportunity both to have it destroyed and to
add to the entertainment.

'I expect them 'acks just got tired and
went 'ome before it 'appened,' Cheadle declared. 'After all, seen one firework display,
you've seen 'em all, 'aven't you?'

Another joke. The pair smiled again. But
he was probably right.

'We got to put a stop to this Quicksilver
business right off if we don't want no more
mayhem,' announced Cheadle, getting back
to business. He paused and smoothed his
side whiskers thoughtfully. 'Thing is, do we
trust the divisionals to do the job? Or does
we do it ourselves?'

The trio exchanged grimacing glances.
Some choice.

'Picture one says you go out there now

and arrest this man.' He glanced from Best, who was fighting to keep his eyes open, to Littlechild, who was using the office wall as a prop to stop himself from falling over.

'Picture two says we send a telegram to Wood Green and get them to send their *best* divisional detectives to watch the place until you get there tomorrow – an' act only if they sees him on the move and up to anything suspicious.'

There was a moment's silence. Certainly, neither picture appealed to Best. He doubted whether he could keep awake for another cab, train and cab journey. He desperately needed to lie down. On the other hand – trusting it to the divisionals! Besides, he wanted to be there, bag the man who had caused him all this worry and woe.

Best and Littlechild looked at each other.

'We'll go now,' they said in unison.

Perusal of Grimes's file had stirred Littlechild's memory some more.

'He wasn't your usual run of villain, I recall. He was quite educated. Had something about him, you know.'

'But did you catch him bang to rights?'

'Oh, yes. No question. He was in his shop, I remember – he was a tailor – when we raided it. Right there, in his cellar, we found all the makings hidden under the floorboards and between the joists: lead, lamp black, plaster of Paris, files, clamps, brushes, a pair of bellows – the lot.

'Hidden among some coal, there was a bag of coins: half crowns, florins, five shilling pieces and a few sovereigns and five pound coins. Some of them were good – for the patterns, of course – but most were counterfeit.'

'Unusual – doing such a selection.'

'Yes. I suppose so.'

Many coiners stuck to the lower denominations because they were easier both to make and to pass. People were less likely to test 'ring' the smaller values and they could be slipped in among 'good' stuff.

Their train had just left Hornsey Station. Best got up and stretched his arms and legs.

'They were impressive specimens, too.' Littlechild frowned. 'One odd thing though, we couldn't find any chemicals or plating solutions anywhere on the premises.'

'He wouldn't cough to where they were?'

'No. Insisted he knew nothing about any of it but couldn't explain what it was all doing there. He was the only one with keys.'

Best felt wide awake in a weird, far off sort of way as they drew into Wood Green station.

'It's only five minutes away,' said Archie, the stocky divisional man sent to meet them. 'Ain't worth getting a cab.'

Divisional men were great walkers. Had to

be. But Best and Littlechild were in no mood for exercise. Even in a cab the journey up Station Road and Green Lanes proved quite a trot, but the evening was turning golden and the pleasant, leafy surroundings helped to perk them up.

Best expected to stop at some railway cottages or an old farm building, so the grandness of Mrs Grimes's abode came as something of a shock.

Standing back from a green, behind tall railings, stood a long, red-brick three-storey building overlooking wide and well-kept lawns and ornamental gardens.

The pantiled roof was punctuated by tall Tudor-style chimneys and, to either side of a central turreted gateway, marched half a dozen smaller but still imposing decorative arched entrances.

A handsome, gilt-lettered board proclaimed that these were the Fishmongers and Poulterers Almshouses. Would that I live somewhere this grand when I am old, thought Best.

'We got a lot of these sort of places around here,' confided Archie. 'Somewhere for the rich to give their money so they don't feel so guilty.'

Mrs Grimes lived at number 4. She took some time to answer her door and, when she did, they realized why. Her eyes were bright and enquiring and her face was not unduly lined but she was leaning heavily on two walking sticks and panting with the effort of getting to her front door.

'Mrs Grimes?' Best enquired doffing his hat.

'Who wants to know?'

'We're friends of your son and would like to have a word with him if he's here?'

She gazed at the detective inspector with ill-concealed contempt. 'You can't be that good friends,' she spat.

Best was too tired to prevaricate. 'Why not?' he snapped.

'Because he's dead. That's why,' she snapped back and shut the door.

Fourteen

It had taken some effort to persuade Mrs Grimes to open her door to them again.

'He was let out early because he was sick,' she said dully. 'He went in a healthy man and came out dying!' She glared at Littlechild and added, 'And it was all your fault.'

The inspector had been watching her sympathetically but he now held up his hand. 'Just a minute, Mrs Grimes. It wasn't my fault that your son was coining.'

'He wasn't.'

'How can you be sure of that?'

' 'E told me. Swore to me.'

'Sons sometimes tell lies to their mothers so as not to upset them.'

'On his death bed?'

What could one say to that? Fortunately, Littlechild didn't try. There was silence for a moment.

Littlechild, who sat opposite her in her sparsely furnished living room, inclined his head and enquired gently, 'Did he by any chance explain what all that coining tackle was doing in his cellar?'

' 'E didn't know. 'E swore to God 'e didn't know. 'E was going to try to find out – but 'e was too ill and 'e died before 'e could.'

'You see, Mrs Grimes,' said Best gently, 'we don't have any record of his death at the Convict Office.'

She gave him a withering look. 'That's not my fault!'

'Have you got a death certificate?'

'Course I 'ave. I 'ad to bury 'im, didn't I?' She pointed one of her sticks at a dark wood box on the sideboard. 'Fetch me that chest.'

Best brought it to her and, digging about whilst muttering to herself about the stupidity of policemen, she pulled out the narrow parchment certificate.

It revealed the cause of death as tuberculosis and gave the date of death as 22nd

July 1880. Almost a month ago.

'Where's his wife?' asked Littlechild.

'Left the country. Took the little girl with 'er.' She kept her sad eyes resolutely on the box as she spoke.

Eventually, she broke the silence which followed by admitting, 'She didn't go straight away. She wrote to 'im and visited 'im for quite a bit and she was faithful, give 'er that. But then she got fed up with it all and went back to Italy. Took little Mary with her.'

There was another silence. Best was too exhausted to react to more sorrow.

She glanced up at the two men and suddenly softened. 'You two lads look as if a good night's sleep wouldn't do you no harm. Do you fancy a cup of tea – or maybe something stronger?' She nodded over at a bottle of cheap gin. 'That keeps me going – gives a bit of comfort.'

They accepted the second option gratefully and were bidden to help themselves. Her sudden change of heart after the tirade of hate at the door was a turnabout familiar to both men. Elderly, lonely people were usually grateful for any company, particularly that with which they could discuss departed loved ones, no matter what the context. Besides, they couldn't always find the energy to sustain anger.

'I expect you 'adn't 'eard because he

wasn't due to report again until this week,' she revealed quietly. 'They let him do it by letter 'cos he was sick.' She levered herself into a more comfortable position. 'Matter of fact that's what I thought you was here about. Funny, ain't it?' she asked.

Not very, thought Best.

Best was grateful that Wood Green police station was only a short way further up the High Road.

So as not to spoil the tone of this newly-colonised middle class district, the architects of the brick, two-storey building, which stood on the corner of residential Nightingale Road, had clearly done their best to ensure it resembled a modest villa.

Once there, Best wrote out a telegram to Cheadle informing him of the death of Grimes and confirming that they had seen the death certificate. It was not unknown for wanted men to arrange for their own temporary demise, so police had to be sure.

He had to write fast. A mounted messenger was due to leave for Tottenham Police Station, which was connected to the telegraph system.

The lines must have been clear with Cheadle waiting at Scotland Yard because the messenger brought back a reply, which stated: 'Best, stay at Wood Green overnight. Smith will arrive tomorrow morning re

141

other business. Littlechild, go home.'

All right for some, thought Best.

Chilton House was a three-storey, tawny London-brick villa behind a gated entrance which sat well back from the pavement.

It wasn't a huge house, thought Best, but it was quite substantial. The stone steps which led to a colonnaded porch and the white limestone trims around the windows gave it a more expensive air than its neighbours. Indeed, he guessed, it was of sufficient rateable value to grant the owner the right to vote – should they be a man, of course. Clearly, Miss Maud Forrest was, at the very least, comfortable.

A white, gravel path circled a small, ornamental flower plot before reaching the entrance in front of which stood a glossy, black brougham van. Between the shafts, an equally glossy black stallion waited patiently. Discreetly inscribed in gold letters on the van's side were the words: Jacob Finbury, Funeral Furnishers and Mourning Outfitters.

Had it not been for the van's presence, Best and Smith would have gained the impression that no one was at home. It was some time before they received a response to their ring on the doorbell. Eventually it came in the form of a stout, flustered-looking, middle-aged woman drying her hands on her apron.

She looked at them enquiringly then de-manded bluntly, 'Yes? Who's callin', please?'

'Mr Best and Mr Smith who were at the palace when Alice took ill,' said Best. 'Just come to pay our respects,' he added piously.

No point in getting the whole neigh-bourhood gossiping before they had the results of the pill analysis.

The woman frowned in concentration as she memorized what they were saying, her lips moving and head nodding as she did so. Then she turned abruptly and walked away.

Best and Smith exchanged amused glan-ces.

'Not been attending her etiquette lessons at Miss Dogood's Academy, I see,' muttered Best.

She soon returned to say, 'You're please to come in 'ere.' She stood back from the door and awkwardly directed them to a hand-some but fussily-furnished drawing room.

'Miss Forrest is bein' measured and outfitted,' she announced. 'An' she says to tell you that she'll come as soon as she can and to please make yourselves comfortable.'

She was visibly relieved to have got that all out and was about to leave when Best mur-mured, 'This is all such a sad business.'

The woman looked confused.

'Oh, er, yes...' she said, pushing a damp strand of greying hair behind her ear. She hesitated, unsure of what was expected next.

'You have our condolences,' he added.

'Oh, I never knew 'er,' she exclaimed, shaking her head. 'I just come in from the agency, to 'elp out.' She hovered uncertainly. 'This is my first time 'ere...'

'Well, you've been a great help,' Best assured her as he settled into one of the rose-bedecked armchairs.

The world was looking rosier today as well, Best admitted. He'd had a good night's sleep in the bed of a constable who had been called home to see his dying mother. The mattress had been a biscuit and the room above the police station barracklike, but he had been too tired to care.

'Seems as if there was no other servants,' he said to Smith when the woman had gone. 'You'd think there would at least be a cleaner in a place this size? Especially as Miss Forrest claims—'

Best stopped as he spotted Miss Forrest framed in the doorway. How much had she heard? He was becoming careless.

He leaped to his feet and went towards her with his hand outstretched and a reverent look on his face. 'We are so sorry to intrude at such a time,' he murmured indicating the funeral brougham outside the window.

She nodded her head rather awkwardly, as though formal niceties unsettled her, particularly when coming from a policeman. Best had heard that northerners thought southerners 'fussy' and 'smarmy' but also that Geordies were usually very friendly.

'I'm trying to give Alice a good send-off,' she said suddenly, as though she had been accused of something untoward. 'We were like sisters, you know.'

'Of course, of course. Absolutely natural you should want to do your best for her.'

Was this guilt or just sheer awkwardness? Clearly, soft words and charm were not likely to work here, Best decided. Straightforwardness, or at least the appearance of straightforwardness, would have to be the order of the day.

Miss Forrest was wearing a deep black barathea dress which hung a little loosely on her lean body. A row of pins down the left side were evidence of an attempt to rectify this problem. Doubtless, a matching row was scheduled for the right hand side but she'd clearly thought their visit important enough to break off her fitting.

She indicated that Best should sit down again and drew up an upright chair opposite him. Her mourning outfit, he noticed, was completed with a lacy black collar, matching gloves and a jet necklace and earrings. The full regalia. To impress whom?

'Are Alice's relatives coming down for the funeral?' he asked.

'Oh, no,' Maud said quickly, then she pulled herself up. 'Well, she didn't have any, did she? Not any very close anyway – and it's such a long way from Newcastle...'

'What made you come all the way down here?' Best enquired politely.

'My sister lived here, didn't she.'

Best had already noticed the woman's curious habit of speaking as if he should know the answers. As if everyone must. Maybe this was the result of living in a small village where everyone did, indeed, know everything about you? Maybe this was a Tyneside way of speech?

'Married a southerner, didn't she.'

Her tone suggested that this was only one remove from being sold into white slavery. Best realized she'd spoken in the past tense.

'You said "lived". Where is she now?'

Maud bowed her head and tears sprang into her eyes, but she fought them back.

'Dead too, isn't she!' She shook her head in almost angry disbelief. 'Would you gainsay it? We'd only just sold the old house up there and bought the new one down here, and she took ill with pneumonia and there she was dead – within a week! My only relative gone!'

She shivered and wrapped her arms around her body in a gesture of self-comfort. 'Family weakness, you know – the chest.'

'So now the only person you've got is your brother-in-law?'

The brother-in-law had quickly assumed a certain importance in Best's mind. If Maud was as wealthy as her gold brooch, diamond ring and house-owning status suggested, this brother-in-law, this only remaining relative of sorts, might not have fancied his inheritance being diluted.

'Oh, no,' she exclaimed as if he ought to know. 'He's gone as well, has he not! Ten years ago. Heart. That's why our Ena wanted me to come south, wasn't it.'

'Your new neighbours,' said Best encouragingly, 'are they friendly?'

Her answer was surprisingly waspish. 'What them! Course not. They're typical southerners!' She stopped and drew back a little. 'Well,' she said more mildly, 'I suppose they've said "Good morning" now and then.' She sighed. 'It takes time, I know.'

Best resisted the urge to spring to the defence of southerners, and instead cleared his throat and murmured, 'Of course. Wherever you are.'

'Did Alice have any friends or relatives down here?'

'Oh, no.' There was a certain satisfaction in her voice. 'There was just the two of us.'

He leaned forward and enquired casually, 'No sweethearts or anything?'

Her eyes widened in astonishment at the

question. 'Why no, man!' Uncertainty crept into her eyes. 'What did you ask me that for?'

'With sudden death we have to ask a few questions,' he assured her apologetically. 'We have to get the full picture of the situation.'

'But she had a heart attack – you said!'

'We said we thought she might have had a heart attack. We didn't know for certain until after the post mortem.'

She stared at him aghast. 'Alice wouldn't have wanted to be cut up by strangers!'

'We had no choice,' Best murmured patting her hand. 'But they were very respectful – and tidied her up afterwards.'

He took a deep breath, might as well get on with it. He'd kept it back so as to get as much information out of her as possible in case she collapsed at the news. He leaned forward and said, 'Look, I've something to tell you.'

She frowned, glancing perplexedly from one man to the other. 'What d'you mean?'

Her eyes, he noticed, were red-rimmed and her face blotchy from crying. Poor woman. And he was about to make it worse. But – no niceties.

'Well, come on, man,' she said bluntly. 'What is it you have to say?'

All right. If that's what you want. 'Just that the pathologist is not happy with the result

148

of his post mortem,' he said equally bluntly.

'Not happy? What do you mean? What are you talkin' about, man? If he's not happy he should do it again!'

'Ah, no. I see that I haven't made myself quite clear. Forgive me.'

She gazed at him implacably.

'What I mean is, that we have found signs that her death may not have been from natural causes.'

Her eyes widened and her hand flew to her mouth. 'Signs? What signs?'

If she was guilty of anything she was making a poor do of hiding it by responding to 'signs' rather than 'causes of death'.

Best shrugged. 'I don't know. It's all too technical for me, I'm afraid.' No it wasn't. When they'd opened up the stomach the stench of bitter almonds had billowed up like a fog from the river. 'It's just suspicions at the moment, you understand. We have to wait for the results of further tests.'

'But, but that's stupid! I mean...'

'It may be,' he said coldly. 'But we've got to act on this, you understand,' he said firmly. 'So what it means to you is that we'll have to hold the burial back for a while.'

'No!' she exclaimed. 'You can't do that!'

Oh really, why not? he wondered.

'Not in this heat. We can't do that to poor Alice.'

'Meanwhile, if you could help us get this

thing sorted out,' Best continued in the businesslike, steamroller manner he had decided was the best option with this woman, 'you will be able to bury your friend all the sooner.'

He was startled to hear a sob burst suddenly from the woman's stringy throat. A torrent of tears began streaming down her angular face. When the tough ones broke they usually went all the way, exhausted by all that holding back. If this were genuine, a touch of kindness now should complete the process.

He reached forward and patted her hand. She looked down as he did so as though not believing that someone had touched her. 'Will you do that for us, Miss Forrest? We would be most grateful.'

She nodded speechlessly as he handed her his clean handkerchief.

'Quicker done, quicker cleared up.'

But not too quick, he thought, we've got to get those poison test results back first.

Fifteen

The goods on offer spilled outside the shops and in some cases right across the pavement: shiny pans, exotic bird cages, carcasses of lamb, glossy fruit and colourful vegetables. Delivery vans and carts still cluttered the kerbside and shopkeepers were putting finishing touches to their displays.

'Commerce Road,' murmured Best. 'Well, they gave it the right name, didn't they?'

He held a list of the establishments patronized by Alice and Maud. With luck, they might offer some clues as to any contacts Alice might have made in the area. The neighbours had been friendly enough when approached but verified Maud's assertion that they never exchanged more than the occasional 'Good morning' with the newcomers. At present, it almost seemed as though neither woman knew anyone at all.

If that were really so, how were they going to trace the murderer, never mind get a hint of a possible motive? Up to now, there seemed no reason why *anyone* should want Alice dead.

Maud would have had the opportunity, but why should she want to kill her help and only companion of many years? By her account the woman was a dear friend. What's more, Alice had no money. Maud had shown them Alice's savings book, which held a princely £4.10s. Nothing to the likes of a woman like Maud.

As far as they could yet discover, Alice's life had not been insured. If it had been, the policy would soon surface along with the claimant and if the company suspected anything they would soon be investigating and informing the police.

When calling on the neighbours, Best and Smith had not announced themselves as police officers, merely hinted that they were representatives of an insurance company searching for information and for possible benefactors.

This, Best had found, was a sure way to bring 'relatives and friends' out of the woodwork. Quite often they turned out to be bogus, but also, quite often, police learned something new during the exercise.

A close look at Maud's financial situation might reveal something. Was she as secure as she appeared to be? Even if not, why would that give her a motive for killing Alice?

Commerce Road and Finsbury Road, which crossed it two thirds of the way up, proved to be a thriving residential shopping centre with the usual mix of retailers catering for the domestic needs of a neighbourhood aspiring to middle-class gentility.

On the greengrocer's laden trestles, exotic foreign fruits such as figs, peaches and pomegranates sat side by side with crisp Cox's Orange Pippins. At the two butchers', pheasants vied with mutton and the fishmonger offered lobsters as well as North Sea cod.

Appetizing aromas were coming from Bennet's High Class Bakers and Confectioners which offered 'Choice Desserts on the shortest notice' in addition to everyday Maid of Honour Tarts.

Best could not imagine Alice and Maud wanting 'choice desserts' for fancy dinner parties, but the baker's was on his list so they began there. The fact that there was a tea shop attached also influenced his decision. He and Smith could partake of a scrumptious pastry while chatting casually to the waitress whose name, they soon discovered, was Emmy.

It turned out to be a good move. The hour was still early and Emmy had time to spare, particularly for such a presentable pair of gentlemen.

'What's happening about Quicksilver?'

Best asked Smith after she had taken their order.

'Cheadle has sent Sergeant Lansdowne out to Pentonville to see Grimes's old cell mates. He reckons he might have given someone else the idea of quoting poems. But he wants us to keep an eye on old Mrs Grimes to see if we can get anything more from her. Find out whether there are any relatives or mates "in the picture" who might be bent on revenge.'

Best looked skywards. 'Bit far-fetched, isn't it? You'd have to be a good mate to do that. You could be hanged for setting off an explosion like that.'

Smith nodded. 'But they can't think of nothing else to do until they get something more from Major Majendie – or receive another threat.'

Little Emmy, the waitress-cum-shop assistant was so young and innocent-looking in her simple dark dress and white, frilly apron, she could be a mere child playing shops. But she was not overawed by her responsibilities.

Her blend of concentrated determination and innocence reminded him of Mary Jane when she had played shops and dragooned him into acting as the difficult customer. He sighed; poor girl must be wondering where he had got to.

This Emmy must be the baker's daughter,

Best decided. His guess was confirmed when the man himself appeared with a tray of bread rolls.

Like her, he had fair, crinkly hair, a stocky build, pale blue eyes and a bustling way of walking as though his life was one of non-stop activity – which it probably was.

Emmy busied her way over to their table to place their coffee and pastries before them. Best smiled up at her and Smith winked his thanks. She blushed, clearly un-used to attentions from such well-set-up gentlemen.

It was obvious that the boyishly handsome Smith had made an impression by the way Emmy kept her eyes averted as she swiftly unloaded a tray of sugar buns into the counter display shelves.

'These,' Best called across to her after a decent interval, 'are the best almond slices.' He licked his lips. 'Every bit as good as we were told they would be.'

Emmy smiled acknowledgement in an uncomprehending manner.

'They certainly are,' Smith agreed. 'Just like poor old Miss Maud said they would be.'

When that brought no response, he added, 'Miss Maud Forrest. I think her maid, Miss Alice, used to come here to place their order.'

'Oh, yeh,' said Emmy, relieved at being

able to grasp what they were talking about. 'Miss Forrest is a good customer.' She laughed conspiratorially and confided, 'They don't half eat a lot of cakes.' She paused and shook her head and frowned. 'But I can't always tell what Miss Alice is sayin', can you?'

Best nodded his sympathy. 'Difficult accent to understand.' He shook his head gravely. 'Sad business about Miss Alice.'

The girl looked puzzled.

Oh good, she didn't know.

'What d'you mean?'

'She's dead.'

'Dead!' Emmy ceased her ladling of iced tarts and stood immobile, tongs upended and mouth agape.

'Yes,' Smith broke in, 'up at the palace the day before yesterday when the police fête was on.'

The girl's eyes widened. 'But, but ... she was in here just...'

'She was riding on one of those new galloper merry-go-rounds when she fell forward,' Smith went on, leaning forward, almost aping her fall, which Best thought was over-egging the pudding somewhat. But the lad was learning. He had the girl transfixed. 'She was hanging down from the saddle and people were screaming but the roundabout kept going round and round and her head began dragging on the ground and bouncing.'

Emmy's hand went to her mouth and a tiny cry escaped her lips.

'The roustabouts couldn't hear her, you see – for the noise of the music and the steam engine,' Best put in, then crunched into his almond slice and left Smith to complete the picture.

Wisely, the young sergeant decided it was time to put a damper on the dramatics. No sense in having the girl go into hysterics. 'Of course, they stopped the roundabout in the end,' he said quietly, then paused. He added even more soberly, 'Her heart, they think it was.' He patted the left side of his chest.

A young woman with two bouncy children entered the shop and began pointing to their choice of cakes. But Emmy still stood transfixed, her mouth open and eyes wide.

'Excuse me?' the woman said.

Emmy's eyes were still on Best who pointed the stunned girl's gaze towards the customer. She turned towards her unseeingly but was brought round by the woman's impatient glance.

They had her now. The rest should be easy.

'Miss Alice said our baking reminded them of home,' Emmy said when the customer had gone.

'Well,' said Best softly, 'that must have been a great comfort to them. They hadn't been here long. Didn't know anyone. Very sad. They must have been a bit lonely.'

Emmy nodded uncertainly. She was clearly still stunned and wanted to talk more but Best got up, thanked the girl, paid her and turned to leave.

Smith was puzzled by Best's urgency. Why go now when they had her in the palm of their hands? He opened his mouth to ask another question but was silenced by a look and closed it again.

'Later,' whispered Best as they reached the street. 'Leave her wanting more.' He grinned at Smith. 'Give her time to think.'

They continued their quest at the butchers' and fishmonger's, tea merchant's and grocer's and came to the conclusion that Alice and Maud had a sweet tooth and very healthy appetites. As well as cakes and tarts from the baker's, they were partial to large joints of beef and legs of lamb, kippers, mussels and Dover sole, jellies and blancmange, and ginger parkin.

The shopkeepers had noticed little about Alice except that she was quite friendly, if a bit abrupt and difficult to understand, and that they seemed to eat a lot considering they were only two women living alone. Certainly they couldn't remember seeing her in company with anyone else, but shopkeepers were probably too busy to absorb the social nuances of their customers' lives.

The tea merchant, who was offering the New Seasons Blends from Lipton's Tea Gardens in sunny Ceylon, proved a little more helpful. His wares were more limited so perhaps they took less of his attention. He imagined he had noticed Alice chatting to a cabman once or twice. But this was a street alive with carts and vans delivering and cabs and dog carts ferrying customers – so he could have been mistaken.

'Right,' said Best as they left. 'It's time we got some humbugs.' He headed back down Commerce Road, then stopped and entered Bennet's, High Class Bakers and Confectioners, where he ordered a quarter of a pound of rum and butter drops.

Emmy was obviously pleased to see them again and eager to talk.

'Can't get over it,' she kept saying. 'That poor woman, dying like that.'

Best inclined his head in agreement. 'Sad business. And with no friends down here to mourn her either.'

Emmy paused in her measuring out of the drops. 'No, excepting for that cabbie,' she said. 'Course you couldn't say he was a friend, could you? But it was always the same fella she had waiting outside.'

'Oh, really?' said Best calmly accepting the paper bag of sweets. 'He may be able to help us.' He paused. 'Could you describe him, do you think?'

He wasn't hopeful. Members of the public were hopeless at descriptions, even of their loved ones. Sometimes they even managed to get the colour of their eyes wrong.

'Oh, yes,' said Emmy, confidently, 'he was that one-eyed bloke who stands over in Station Road. The one with the patches on the side of his cab.'

Smith and Best exchanged wide-eyed glances.

'Well done,' Best nodded. 'That could be quite helpful.'

Smith leaned forward and said, 'Thank you, Emmy.' And she blushed again. 'This is just between us for the moment. All right?'

She nodded, transfixed by Smith's blue eyes and beguiling smile.

'I only noticed because I thought it was funny how she still had some of the stuff delivered when they could have taken it all back with them – if they was goin' home then, that is.'

How interesting, thought Best. Some of the stuff, and if they were going home. He couldn't have put it better himself. Alice, it seemed, had a fella and had been on the fiddle. Matters were taking on a different hue – definitely a rosier one for them anyway.

Sixteen

A black eyepatch gives some men a rakish and jaunty air – but the one-eyed cabbie wasn't one of them.

Runt of the litter was more the phrase that came to Best's mind as he spotted him, alongside the row of cabs waiting down the road from Wood Green Railway Station.

If he was Alice's paramour she certainly hadn't chosen him for his looks.

As Best approached, the cabbie had a final puff on his clay pipe, tapped the dottle into the gutter and climbed nimbly up on to the seat of his growler.

Clearly, a train was due. He must be hoping that there would more trade than could be handled by the cabs licensed to stand directly outside the station. Also, that sufficient passengers would require the additional luggage space offered by even a shabby four-wheeler like his.

When Best stopped before him and held up his hand, the one-eyed cabbie shook his head and said out of the corner of his mouth, 'Sorry mate. Not my turn – be more

161

than my life's worth...'

'Police,' said Best showing his identification. 'I want a word.'

He looked indignant.

'Why me?' he exclaimed. 'I ain't done nothing!' He frowned. 'Oh, I know. It was that woman yesterday complaining. You can tell her *she* owes *me*! Miserable cow!'

'Nobody's complained,' Best assured him. 'I just need a word. Some information you can help me with – local knowledge.'

The cabs ahead began to move forward. Obviously, the train had arrived. Drivers in the queue behind voiced their objections to being held up. Some started pulling out to overtake. 'Not just now, mate,' he pleaded. 'There's work up there...'

Best pointed off to the right in the direction of a plot of ornamental gardens. 'Over there,' he commanded in a brook-no-argument manner as he pulled himself on board, 'into Avenue Gardens. Then stop on the left.'

The cabbie watched sadly as his fellow cabmen began coming back down the road carrying passengers, but Best knew he wouldn't dare refuse. The police controlled the cab trade whether the cabbies liked it or not, and they didn't much. Being a Blucher (last on the field at the railway station, like the general of the same name was at Waterloo) he probably couldn't afford any

162

suspension of business.

'You needn't worry,' Best assured him, as they halted by the low railings of the ornamental gardens typical of leafy, sedate Wood Green, 'I only want to ask you about one of your customers. There's been no complaint about your cab.' His glance over the moth-eaten upholstery and grimy woodwork implied that there could be, if...

'Didn't think there could be.' He shrugged as he climbed down from his box.

Close up, he seemed taller. He was quite neat about the neck and the black bowler was almost new. When he took if off to wipe his brow, Best caught a pungent whiff of cedar-wood pomade from the man's black, sleek wavy hair. A ladies' man – despite his obvious drawback? Could be.

A one-armed man had once revealed to Best that, far from being a disadvantage, his disability was a positive asset with the ladies. Firstly, it engaged their sympathies while at the same time putting them off their guard, allowing him to get nearer without frightening them off.

Best ushered him to a garden bench and sat alongside him on his left – his good side.

'First of all,' said Best, 'what's your name?'

'Arthur, Arthur Herring.' He paused. 'But there's nothing fishy about me.'

How often had he cracked that one? Best wondered. However, the detective inspector always believed in doing things the easy way, if at all possible, so he laughed, slapped his thigh and exclaimed, 'I hope not, Arthur! I hope not!'

'You ain't going to keep me long are you?' Arthur pleaded. 'I 'aven't even made my hiring yet.'

Ah, so even this shabby cab was not his own. He was a bailee, hiring the vehicle for so much a day. Best didn't like making things any harder for a working man. On the other hand...

'Quicker we get down to business...' he reassured him. Then he added some pressure: 'And the quicker you help me with some information, the sooner you'll get back on the rank.'

'Right,' said Arthur, shifting uneasily in his seat. Closer, he was also wily, ferrety and quick-eyed. Even though he possessed only one of the latter, it seemed to be darting everywhere.

He could be wrong, but Best got the impression that Arthur had no idea what this was all about.

'What I want to ask you about is one of your regular customers. A lady.'

'Regular?' He was puzzled. 'Don't have many of those.'

'This one's called Alice.'

Arthur scratched his head, sending waves of cedar wood Best's way. 'Alice...?'

'Servant of Maud Forrest up at Chilton House. I've been told she used to hire you sometimes when she went shopping in Commerce Road...'

Best left that hanging in the air. There was a long pause while Arthur's eye continued darting about, before it eventually came to rest on the inspector.

'Oh yes. Now I recalls.' He spread his hands in explanatory style. 'You carry so many, it gets a bit confusing.'

'Alice,' said Best again.

'Right. Right. A little woman? That her?'

Best nodded. 'Maybe having only one eye makes it harder to get a good look at people?' he said quietly.

He sensed that Arthur was about to agree but then got the drift and stopped himself.

'With driving as well.' Best paused. 'I mean, is it safe? You not being able to see on one side?'

'Oh, yeh! Course it is!'

Best sucked his teeth. 'I mean,' he said, applying the pressure a bit more, 'especially the *right* eye. When you pull out from the rank you can't see what's coming, can you?'

'Yes, I can! Yes, I can! I've never had no accident!' He sounded desperate now. 'I'm used to it, ain't I? Been like this since I was a kid and been driving since I was ten.'

The silence which Best had allowed to grow after his veiled threats began to bear

165

fruit.

'I'm remembering much more about the lady now,' Arthur Herring confided. 'As I said, she's little ... and skinny, speaks her mind, and has a funny accent.'

'Tyneside,' said Best.

'Er, yeh,' Arthur nodded, now eager to spill anything he knew.

'First time I picked her up was on a Monday afternoon in Commerce Road. I was on the way back to Station Road to meet up with the four twenty-seven,' he explained. 'After that, if I was about on Monday, Wednesday and Friday afternoons around quarter past four, I would pick her up and drive her 'ome.'

'Isn't Commerce Road a long way from Station Road?'

'Oh, yeh. I only goes to the station on days and days about. Take turns with the other Bluchers.'

'So, what was Alice like?'

'Like I said, little and had a funny accent. Tipped not bad for a woman.'

Best said nothing. Nervous people always felt bound to fill silences.

'Didn't say much at first. She didn't take to any soft talk, I'll tell you that. But she got a bit more friendly when I h'understood 'er better.'

'Ah, your winning southern ways didn't go down well at first then?'

He wasn't sure how to take that but eventually grinned and admitted, 'She said southerners was too "fussy" for her.'

He paused. 'It's hard to chat natural-like to folk when you're perched up there, you knows–' he nodded at the driver's box high above the forecarriage – 'an' they're inside.'

There was another short silence. Then Arthur slowly turned his head right around giving Best a full view of the good eye and the eye patch. 'What d'you mean?' he said. 'What *was* she like?'

Detective Sergeant Smith just happened to be passing Chilton House in a hansom cab when the weary cleaning lady emerged, shopping list in hand.

He stopped the cab a little way down the road, out of eyeshot of the villa.

'Like a lift?' he called down to her. 'You look a bit tired.'

The woman stopped and gazed up at him, quite startled that anyone should notice that she was tired, much less offer to save her feet.

'Remember me?' Smith continued cheerfully as he opened the knee flap to admit her. 'We came to see Miss Forrest this morning.'

His behaving as though her acceptance was a foregone conclusion, as Best had taught him to do, overcame her uncertainty.

She climbed bemusedly aboard.

'Big house to keep clean, all on your own, that one,' he said.

She nodded breathlessly.

'You doing the shopping as well?'

She nodded again.

'Well, I'm off to Commerce Road. Is that any good to you?'

She nodded again. 'Yes, save my poor old legs, that will.'

'Save your legs more if they got the tradesmen to call, wouldn't it?'

She shook her head. 'Miss Forrest won't have them calling. Says she wants some black pudding and the butcher only brings it if it's been ordered.'

She paused, uncertain as to whether she ought to be sharing Miss Forrest's shopping secrets with this young man. Then, she shrugged. 'Anyway, she doesn't want to be bothered with any more callers just now. So, her being in mourning an 'all, I'm to take back what she needs.'

'Oh, understandable, I suppose. Being in mourning and all.'

'Yeh.' She shrugged again before adding mischievously, 'She don't mind the jeweller coming calling though.' She waved an envelope in the air.

Well, well. Jeweller. Now why would that be?

'Oh, I expect she needs a bit of jet for her

mourning dress,' Smith said.

'Nah. She's got that.' The cleaning woman paused, then added with a curl of the lip, 'Dunno why she's bothering. Not going to be anybody there, 'cept her and a couple that's paid to be, is there?'

'I suppose she wants to do the right thing.' Smith paused. 'You're right though, it does seem to be an odd time to be buying jewellery. But maybe if it cheers her up – I know it would my wife and—'

'Oh, she's not *buying*,' the woman exclaimed, 'she's *selling*.'

'So,' said Detective Inspector Best, as he inspected his pint at eye level, 'it looks like our Miss Forrest might be in financial difficulties after all.'

Smith nodded. 'The cleaner says she saw her getting a whole pile of jewellery together.'

'Hmm,' mused Best. 'Maybe her bosom friend Alice was rooking her of more than the odd leg of lamb.'

Arthur had eventually admitted to some such chicanery, but swore it had gone no further than petty fraud. A pound of tea here, a dozen eggs there – which he then sold on and shared the profits with Alice.

'Maud learned about it,' Best went on, 'and...'

'Killed her? Why would she do that when

she could just sack her or dock it off her wages?' questioned Smith.

'Right,' nodded Best, 'and why poison? I mean, if it was in anger?'

'Well, some women think it's the only way they can strike out – even against another woman.'

None of it made any sense, Best thought. He contemplated the mutton pie advertised as the Alexandra Tavern's best 'ordinary', and which looked just that.

'There's something here that we're missing,' he said.

They'd been to the police station where a telegram had confirmed the poison test as positive. 'It's time to show our hand.'

'What we need to do,' said Best firmly, 'is to search that house thoroughly and examine Miss Forrest's financial affairs minutely. Let's go and get us a warrant.' He paused and sighed. 'But, of course, you know what would happen the minute we do that?'

Smith nodded. 'It'll get out. Huge crowds will descend on Chilton House and Wood Green Police Station. Terrible rumours will fly. Witnesses will be forewarned ... thinking there's going to be a reward...'

'And we won't be able to move for gentlemen of the press breathing down our necks. Tell you what,' Best said, taking a chance and biting into the pie, 'let's go and talk to Maud again, first. Friendly like.'

Seventeen

Maud, who was pouring tea into rose-sprigged bone china cups, seemed more at ease this time. She looked better, too. The funeral outfitters' sewing needles had clearly been flying, for her mourning dress now fitted snugly around her lean frame.

She had even managed to soften her manner a little. Clearly, thought Best, she was getting over the initial shock of losing her sole companion and was now more herself; hence the tea, which Best readily accepted in the cause of smoothing the way.

He had not, however, got around to breaking the news that the poison test had proved positive.

'The shop assistants all speak well of Alice,' he said kindly. 'They say she was very straightforward to do business with.' He paused and smiled. 'They found her a bit hard to understand at first – the accent, of course. I expect she found them the same?'

Maud nodded. 'I wouldn't be surprised. She was only a simple lass from the country, you know.' She drew herself up. 'At least she was when I found her.'

'Really?' Best waited for more revelations but, when they were not forthcoming, he enquired, 'Did she live with her parents?'

'Oh, no,' Maud exclaimed. 'Never even knew them, did she? She was brought up in the Wykham's Children's Home.' She sniffed. 'Dragged up, more like.'

'How sad.'

'Aye, it was horrible!' she spat out suddenly. 'They treated her like dirt, they did!' She paused, a little embarrassed by her outburst, then added more quietly, 'That's why she was so happy with me, of course. She always said I was her family now.'

'You must be pleased that you gave her some happiness.'

Maud looked away as if surprised and embarrassed by the idea. She plucked uncertainly at the fingers of her lace gloves. 'Oh, aye. I suppose.'

'So, did she never meet her parents?'

She shook her head. 'They died of cholera when she was only just a bairn. That's why she was in the home.'

'No other relatives?'

'No,' she agreed firmly. 'If there were any they kept well out of the way when they were needed.'

Best frowned. 'When was that?'

'When she was growing up of course, man!'

'Oh, yes.'

The woman clearly had a short fuse. But she had had a terrible shock. Or could it be that she was nervous due to fear and guilt?

'Your sympathies do you credit, Miss Forrest,' he murmured.

She stared at him uncertainly. Did she wonder whether he was trying to catch her out – or think this was just more southern smarm?

Eventually, she inclined her head in acknowledgement and offered him some more ginger parkin.

'No more than my duty to a poor orphan, was it? Then, it was just for friendship.' Tears sprang into her eyes and for a moment she really did look bereft.

'Well, you were obviously the only friend she had,' said Best. He then confided, 'We've certainly not been able to track down any more.'

She looked startled that they should have been trying to do so. 'Why should she have any friends down here? We've only just arrived, haven't we?'

Was she relieved that they had not found anybody? Surely not. If she'd done the deed, as he suspected she might have, finding another suspect should be good news. But, he came back to the question yet again, why should she kill her only friend and helpmeet?

'We did manage to speak to Arthur Herring. Didn't we?' Smith reminded him, on cue.

'Oh yes, I forgot,' Best lied. 'Lovely parkin this, Miss Forrest.'

Arthur Herring's name hung in the air until at last Miss Forrest ventured, 'Arthur ...?' She shook her head. 'That name means nowt to me.'

'A cab driver. He used to bring Alice back from her shopping trips.'

'Oh,' nodded Maud. 'That would be why, then. I'd have never seen him, would I? Well, only from a distance.' She paused then rushed on: 'She did love going down there, to them shops, you know.' She sat straighter. 'Not my cup of tea – all that fussing about.'

A note of contempt almost crept into her voice but she clawed it back with an indulgent smile. It was curious, thought Best, that she didn't want to know more about Arthur Herring.

He allowed the ensuing silence to stretch before leaning forward in a confidential manner and saying carefully, 'There's only one other thing I'd like to know.' He paused. 'I don't want to upset you, you understand...'

'Go on, man. Go on!'

'Did you and Alice ever have any money problems?'

'Money problems? What d'you mean?' She pulled irritably at the glove frills. 'How

174

could we? She had none!'

There was a short silence while her dismissive words hung in the air.

Best took a deep breath. 'What I mean is, did you ever find Alice out in any dishonesty?'

She looked at him aghast.

'No! What a terrible idea.'

'It's not unheard of with servants,' Best insisted. 'Just a few coppers here and there ... Not necessarily anything very serious but—'

'Down south it may not be!' she spat out. 'Or with people who are not close like us. But Alice and me. Never!'

'If she hates the south and southerners so much, what is she doing here?' muttered Best, as he and Smith walked back to Wood Green Police Station.

'Do you think she really had no idea she was being rooked?' asked Smith, scratching his head. 'She seems sharp enough to me.'

'Well, it would be wiser not to tell us if she did know, wouldn't it? Might make us suspicious.'

'Oh yes, I suppose so.' He scratched his head again. 'But she's hardly going to kill her over a pound of mincemeat and half a dozen eggs, is she?'

'Oh, I don't know,' said Best. 'These things can wear a person down. Being taken for a fool can enrage a person.'

As they sauntered along the leafy avenue in a companionable silence Smith muttered suddenly, 'A thought has just come to me.'

'Ah. Fire away. We need all the thoughts we can muster here. This is a very puzzling business.'

'Mrs Herring.'

'Is there one?'

'I dunno. But if there *is*...'

'Jealousy? Oh, yes, that's always a good motive. Better than any we've got right now.'

Obtaining the search warrant the following morning proved more time consuming than they had expected. The local magistrates were reluctant to be seen to be giving in easily to arrogant Scotland Yard men.

Then there was the disagreeable idea that a murder could have been committed in these sylvan groves. If such a notion got abroad it would do nothing for the builders and estate agents of ever-expanding Wood Green, one each of whom were represented on the bench of three magistrates.

Consequently, there was much fussing and prevaricating before, pressured by the Clerk of the Court who told them they had no option, they finally gave in and issued a warrant. Best and Smith were thus in need of sustenance before they proceeded to

Chilton House to beard Miss Forrest.

'Odd that her dress wasn't crêpe,' Smith muttered as he finished his spotted dick pudding and Best fished out his cigarettes.

The inspector was used to Smith's occasional odd pronouncements about women's clothes. The lad's mother had taken in washing which had afforded her son an unusual insight into the subject. His knowledge had proved useful on other occasions; crucial even, in the Regent's Canal murder case.

'Don't follow you.'

'Well, she's trying to be respectable, isn't she? And respectable mourning dresses are always made of crêpe, aren't they?'

Best raised his eyebrows. 'Don't know.' What he did know was not to rush the lad when he was slowly teasing odd strands of esoteric information from his brain.

'Well, you remember when we first saw her, she was getting her dress fitted – all them pins down the side?'

Best nodded, 'Y-e-s...'

'It was made of barathea. Which meant it was just an ordinary day dress she was having altered.'

'So? Maybe she doesn't care about being respectable after all?'

'But why didn't it fit her in the first place?'

'She'd lost weight?'

'Huh.' Smith was frowning, struggling for

enlightenment.

'I wish you'd tell me...'

'And why–' Smith banged his spoon handle on the table, as his thoughts crystallized – 'why, does she always wear gloves? Even indoors?'

'Only lacy ones,' Best pointed out. 'Maybe it's a northern habit.' Even to him that didn't ring true. Something was also tugging at the back of his mind. Suddenly, everything slid into place for both of them.

They stared at each other, open-mouthed, and exclaimed in unison, 'Kate Webster!'

'Oh God!' exclaimed Best. 'What fools we are!'

They stumbled to their feet, crashed out of the pub and hailed a growler.

'Chilton House!' Best shouted.

Egged on by the promise of a generous tip, the cabbie made almost as much haste as a sleek new hansom. But it was too late.

There was no answer to their knocking and all appeared deserted beyond the heavy curtains. They noticed that the drawing room now looked somewhat bare of clocks and the smaller, choicer ornaments.

The bird had flown.

Eighteen

'So it wasn't the servant Alice who died, but Maud, the mistress.' Best sighed. He and Smith sat opposite each other in the somewhat denuded Chilton House drawing room.

'And Alice took her place – just like Kate Webster with Mrs Thomas.'

'We should have guessed. It's not that long ago.'

Indeed, it was only eighteen months since servant Kate Webster had quarrelled with her mistress, the reclusive Mrs Thomas of Vine Cottages in Richmond, and attacked her with an axe. She chopped her up, dropped her remains in the Thames and, while selling off the woman's property, pretended to be Mrs Thomas herself. Kate's own friends and aquaintances were informed that she had come into an inheritance.

'I suppose we've had other things on our minds,' Smith comforted. He didn't like to see his old friend and colleague depressed.

Mrs Thomas's remains had soon been

found but were not identified until a neighbour became suspicious of the comings and goings next door and the absence of Mrs Thomas. Kate Webster fled back home to Ireland where she was eventually tracked down. She had sworn that it was not her but a man friend, John Church, who had done the dirty deed.

'The clothes should have told us,' said Smith.

Best nodded. Class and clothes usually came into it somewhere, but he wasn't quite sure what his clothes-conscious colleague was driving at this time.

He remembered that when caught, Kate Webster had still been wearing Mrs Thomas's clothes and jewellery but by the time she appeared in the dock alongside Church, she had been stripped of most but not all of them.

Her jacket was of a shabby cloth trimmed with imitation fur and her dress of a material 'usually favoured by respectable servants', *The Times* had reported snootily. Her hat, however, was stylish and 'quite out of keeping with a servant's position'.

The presumptuous woman was found guilty and hanged.

Smith sighed. 'Alice wore gloves to hide her rough hands and that dress that was being taken in, belonged to her mistress, Maud.'

Best could see they were going to have problems remembering which was which and murmured to himself, 'Maud is the victim, Alice the killer.'

'No wonder she didn't seem at ease as the mistress of the house,' Best said. 'She wasn't.'

'And we thought it was just because she was from the north!'

Best would rather he had not rubbed that in. He felt enough of a fool already. 'Now that we *know*,' he said with a slightly tart emphasis, 'all the pieces fit.'

'But why sell the jewels?' puzzled Smith. 'We've seen how much money there is in Maud's accounts.'

'She might have been having trouble with the signature. That's if she can write at all.'

Best and Smith contemplated each other silently. The prospect of the wrath of Cheadle hung over them like a fog wreathing the Thames' bank on a still and wintry day.

'We're going to have to be clever when we make our report,' Best muttered.

Smith looked doubtful.

'Don't worry, little George Washington,' he continued, 'I don't mean tell outright lies. We just have to find a way to distract the man.'

They stared morosely at the carpet for a while, then said in unison, 'How did she think she could get away with it?'

'No one knew them down here,' Best pointed out. 'Remember, even the people next door weren't sure which was the mistress and which the servant. If there had been any doubts, I expect they probably dismissed them, not wanting to raise anything which might lower the tone.'

'Never thought of that,' said Smith. The prospect of ever owning anything made of bricks and mortar was beyond his imagining. 'And she was very clever,' he admitted. 'She knew she would be recognized in Commerce Road, so she sent the new cleaner down to the shops. Gave us a photograph of them *both together*. That might not have worked – but did.'

'Yes. Yes. All right. Let's not have a wake,' exclaimed Best irritably.

He believed in learning from experience but not in flagellating oneself unnecessarily. Better to occupy yourself finding a cunning way out.

Best smiled in spite of himself. 'You're just a devious foreigner, my lad,' Helen had always teased him. He had told her that foreigners had no choice but to become devious.

'D'you think she was going to try to stick it out?' asked Smith more gingerly. 'Be Maud for ever?'

Best shrugged. 'Who knows?' He pulled at

the ends of his moustaches which were in dire need of a barber's attentions. 'I expect she was seeing how much she might get away with.'

'That accent will be hard to hide,' Smith suggested hopefully.

'Up here, in genteel Wood Green maybe, but not down in the Great Wen.' He gazed at Smith, rolled the rogue ends of his wayward moustache into points, and said, 'What we need to know now is how much Arthur knew. If he has any idea where she might have gone—'

'Or whether he has scarpered with her,' Smith finished for him.

Best and Smith were still rifling through the remaining papers in the mock antique desk in the cosy parlour to the rear of the house, when Smith stiffened and looked up.

'What's that?' he asked.

'What?'

'That noise.'

They stood still and listened. A low murmuring sound met their ears. It grew louder as they entered the hall and walked towards the front of the house and was punctuated by the odd raucous shout.

'Don't open the door!' exclaimed Best suddenly, grasping Smith's outstretched arm. 'In here, come on. Keep your head down.'

They crept into the drawing room, ducking low as they went. When they reached the shelter of the heavy rose damask curtains which framed the front-facing window, they peeked out.

In the gateway was an excited crowd – all staring at the house. The noise grew even louder. The word 'murder' could be discerned and there was much hissing. One or two cheekier souls, overcome by the drama of it all, were starting to edge forward into the grounds.

'Let's get out of here,' hissed Best. 'Keep low,' he whispered. 'Head for the back of the house.'

Once out of the conservatory and into the back garden, they surveyed the possible escape routes.

They contemplated slipping over into one of the adjacent gardens but decided that might not be wise. With all this commotion, the neighbours were bound to be on the alert and, besides, would recognize them from their earlier visit.

Instead, they followed the wide sweep of the garden around the left side of the house, then began creeping foward under the cover of the blackcurrant and gooseberry bushes.

'We'll run for the back of that high hedge,' Best whispered, pointing to the spot where the greenery separated the property from the pavement and the outside world.

'Everyone is staring at the front of the house. They won't notice us.'

Smith wished he could be so sure.

'I'll go first,' Best whispered as they crept forward. 'Wait a moment, then you come. Filter into the crowd. See you down the road.' He was gone.

Smith couldn't quite understand why all this lurking about was necessary. They were in the house legitimately, were even in possession of a search warrant. But if Inspector Best said he had to lurk about in this guilty manner, then he supposed he had no choice.

He watched bemused as his superior officer made an undignified dash for the inside of the hedge, sidled along towards the entrance, then slid behind a man who was straining forwards and upwards trying to see through the sitting-room windows. No one had noticed him. That luck couldn't hold out twice.

Smith counted to twenty then made his run. Just as he had feared, when he reached the hedge a man at the forefront turned his head sharply, frowned and said, 'Hey! What?'

'Looks like there's nobody at 'ome,' muttered Smith as he strode forward and pushed through the crowd. 'So that's where I'm going. Excuse me. My dinner's waiting.'

Always look as though you should be

doing what you are doing, and nobody will stop you, had been one of Best's early instructions. Now, as he strode through the throng, Smith steeled himself to obey three other remembered Bestisms for escaping a possibly hostile crowd: don't look as if you're spoiling for a fight. Don't catch anyone's eye. When you're past, don't look back.

'Couldn't get caught up in all that business,' murmured Best as a pink-cheeked, but relieved, Smith came alongside further up the avenue. 'We need to get after Arthur as quick as we can.'

'But what about the house? They might break in.'

'I doubt it,' said Best. 'They know the police will be here any minute.'

'Will they?'

'Oh, yes. We'll tell the first constable we see and if we don't see any we'll tell the nick. But I expect they know by now anyway.'

Again, Smith wished he felt so sure.

'Ah, here they are,' said Best as a purposeful posse of policemen came marching along the avenue. 'The neighbours will have sent their servants to fetch them. Can't have rabbles in this neighbourhood, can they? Avert your face as they go by.'

'But—' spluttered Smith.

'Do it!' ordered Best.

'He ain't been 'ere today,' announced Eddie, a fair-haired young cabbie heading the secondary queue at the station rank. 'Not that I've seen, anyways.'

'Does he always come when it's his turn?' enquired Best nonchalantly.

The amiable young fellow shrugged. 'Dunno. We comes and goes so don't always see each other.'

When Best asked who actually owned Herring's cab, the other drivers fell into an impromptu conference. Clearly, not all were happy to impart such knowledge to an out-sider.

Best was preparing to come the heavy policeman but there was no need. Eddie soon popped up his head and said, 'Straker's, down the High Street.'

'Whereabouts?'

'On the left goin' up. Can't miss it. Want a ride?'

They could scarcely refuse.

It transpired that Arthur Herring had not been at Straker's that morning either. This was surprising, opined the sharp-eyed Mr Straker, because the fellow needed the money.

Best and Smith glanced at each other, Best miming a gnashing of teeth. Clearly, they had been well and truly caught out. Best was painfully aware that one of the reasons for this was that he had not been working alone.

It wasn't Smith's fault. He had not persuaded Best away from any likely lead nor determined path against his better judgement. It was merely that working with a colleague became just a little too companionable – a bit of a lark – which distracted Best and diluted the necessary sense of urgency. Two heads weren't always better than one.

To neither man's surprise, Arthur Herring also turned out to be not at home at his lodgings at number 2, Railway Terrace.

'He's gone down to get his new licence,' confided his frowzy landlady. 'Should be back soon – if he don't get a sniff of the barmaid's apron first.'

So, there was no point in trying to track the man down. They'd just have to go back later and catch him in. If he came back.

Best wondered whether to instruct the landlady to send Herring down to the nick but thought better of it. If he was already nervous that might drive him right away.

Nothing for it now but to bite the bullet, return to the nick, send a telegram off to Cheadle and face the wrath of the local police. And some wrath it was going to be, they realized, when they saw the crowds gathered around Wood Green Police Station.

Nineteen

'The clerks are drawing up the reward notice.' said Best hurriedly. 'I'm getting copies of the photograph produced and I've sent an enquiry off to the Northumberland Police.'

'So they can tell 'em to let 'er go if they sees 'er?' suggested Cheadle sarcastically. 'Might as well.'

Best said nothing.

He had already suffered back at Wood Green Police Station when the superintendent had suddenly appeared wanting to know just what was going on in his division. Then he had handed Best the telegraph message from Cheadle instructing him to return to the Yard forthwith, leaving Smith and the local detectives to carry on with the murder enquiry.

Not that there was much for them to do. They could only ask the neighbours whether they had seen Alice's departure from Chilton House and track down the cab which must have assisted in her removal. All of which was happening while Best and

189

Smith had been held up by Wood Green worthies, reluctant to grant them a search warrant.

Of course, there was always the possibility that she had left the previous evening and it had been Herring's cab which had taken her away. In which case, the task was going to be that much harder. They'd be left without any leads.

The divisional detectives had set out with a will, obviously anxious to show the Scotland Yard men a thing or two. In any case, tracing the cabbie was, Smith acknowledged, the best use of their talents. They not only had the advantage of local knowledge but could lean on the drivers with threats as to future vehicle inspections and supervision.

This left Smith at a bit of a loose end so he decided to return to No 2 Railway Terrace in the forlorn hope of finding Herring at home.

He wasn't. Neither was his 'landlady'.

Despite the fact that Cheadle was clearly not pleased with Best, he was not as acerbic as expected, even though the plan to distract him with involvement in the chase had failed. The leads were not complex enough for that. It was just down to the classic remedy: first find the cabbie.

'They'll know,' was all Cheadle had

muttered, adding, 'she'll have gone back up north.'

'But they're forewarned up there. She'd realize that.'

'Not to Newcastle, you fool!' the Chief Inspector had exclaimed. 'Just somewhere up north where she'll feel more at 'ome, won't stand out so much – and that seems a long way from 'ere.'

The reason for Cheadle's relative mildness soon became clear.

'We've 'ad another letter,' he admitted.

Ah, the distraction had been provided for him, Best realized with relief. He'd half guessed as much when he'd seen the chaotic jumble of files spread across the desks in the sergeants' room. The frantic search for likely Quicksilver suspects continued.

'Littlechild got nowhere at Pentonville Prison,' Cheadle complained. 'An' the rest of 'em can't come up with nothing about this.' He shoved a small square of blue-lined paper across the desk. 'But seeing as 'ow you're so artistic...'

His jibe didn't carry quite the usual bite. Clearly the man was worried. He and Shore remained in charge of operations while Williamson was away. Vincent, as Director of the CID, only covered policy and organization although – if he got the chance – he liked to dabble in the cases. Something to tell his friends about at his club, no doubt.

Vincent was a far more educated man than any of them. And he could see why Cheadle had not asked him for his opinion, not wanting him to think that they couldn't work it out for themselves.

That was a dangerous game to play. If the delay allowed disaster to happen unchecked ... Old man's pride. Should he be party to it? Did he have a choice?

The note said:

WARNING FOR THOSE CLEVER MEN OF SCOTLAND YARD!!! It won't be so easy for you this time! YOU'LL HAVE TO GUESS THE WHERE AND WHEN OF THE COMING CATASTROPHE!!! But I must be fair – Ha Ha. News from all nations will lead you there.

QUICKSILVER

'Littlechild thinks "News from all nations" might be a quote from a poem or something, but he doesn't know which one,' confessed Cheadle. 'We'd better get that ex-lady friend of yours to 'elp us out if you can't.'

Oh, had we? thought Best. What a nerve the man had. There had to be other, easier ways to do this. But not, Best suspected, ones which would save Cheadle's face in the same way.

'I'll see if I can get hold of her, sir,' Best acquiesced, casually.

'Go on – you've been dying to have a good excuse to see her again.'

Best shrugged. The man was right of course, as usual, but he wasn't going to admit that to the old bugger.

'We've been racking our brains for anything in the news that might fit. Can't find nothing "from all nations". There ain't no international meetings nor exhibitions in London, or nothing. Just things 'appening abroad.' He waved his right hand vaguely outwards to indicate the rest of the world.

Best nodded. 'The Afghan War and the Irish problem.'

'Yeh. That's about it.' Cheadle took a deep breath and pushed himself upright in his chair once more. 'More than one country in that Afghan business.'

'Us, the Indians, the Afghans and the Russians.'

'But that's never *all* nations is it?' complained Cheadle. 'Same with this Irish business. There's us again, of course, the Irish and the Americans – in an outside kind of way.'

'It's a puzzle,' Best admitted. 'Might it be something to do with the newspapers themselves? Where all this news comes to?'

'We thought about that,' Cheadle admitted. 'Can't see it myself. Don't seem to fit. What's he goin' to do? Blow up *The Times* offices?'

'He might,' said Best but agreed it didn't seem to fit. The police wouldn't be sufficiently embarrassed, which seemed to be what Quicksilver wanted. That, and to kill a lot of people.

'So, what we're doin' is trying to find the culprit in those files – and more about that quote.'

Cheadle reached over and retrieved the letter, held it up at arm's length and contemplated it with contempt, as if this might produce the answer or frighten off the perpetrator. 'So you go off and see this Helen woman. But before you does, see Inspector Littlechild. 'E wants a word.'

Herring's neighbours at Railway Terrace described how the 'landlady' had left, carrying a carpet bag, just after Smith and Best had paid their call.

Smith kicked the wall in frustration as he left. They had allowed another bird to fly the coop!

Still, it cleared up one question. No doubt now that Herring was involved.

His landlady had left the cottage on foot and, so far, they had failed to discover who had conveyed Alice away from Chilton House.

At least, Smith thought that was the case, but he could not be sure. One of the local detectives might already be on to something, but either not be sharing his knowledge, or had failed to report back yet.

It was at times like these that Smith longed for the invention of a portable telegraph machine so that fellow officers could pass on information as soon as it was acquired.

Failing that, it would help if they would just equip all police stations with telegraph machines. That would be particularly helpful to Scotland Yard detectives, who had a great need to keep in touch with headquarters, as well as each other.

Smith knew that he'd be even more out of touch if he left Wood Green Police Station now, but he couldn't sit there doing nothing. He decided to try the next, obligatory port of call when chasing suspects; after cab ranks – railway stations.

The photograph of Maud and Alice was still being reproduced by the High Street photographer. But tucked away in the desk at Chilton House, they had discovered a much smaller, rather indistinct picture of the pair when younger. It showed a pensive Maud and a laughing Alice in front of a seaside backdrop.

Wood Green's fussy little ticket collector did not recall seeing anyone resembling the laughing Alice, accompanied with heavy luggage, either earlier that day or the evening before. Neither did the grizzled old station master.

But, as they both pointed out, it was such a busy station. Smith could appreciate what they meant. Wood Green catered not only for local line traffic but main line as well.

He soldiered on, determinedly. Wood Green was also home to Palace Gates railway station which served the new line taking clerks and dockers (on special cheap workmen's trains) to the City and the docks in the mornings and brought them back again in the evenings. In between, it ferried its pleasure-bound Ally Pally customers. But he had no luck there – nor further down the line at Green Lanes Station.

So, what next? Go back and look around Chilton House again? Return to Railway Terrace and ask the neighbours some more questions? Neither prospect seemed promising.

He perched fretfully on a bench on Green Lanes downline platform and proceeded to have a good, quiet think.

But it was no good. Nothing emerged. No instant answer, no dawning realization, no flash of inspiration.

Dusk melted into darkness and the air grew chilly. He chaffed his hands together and slapped his arms to warm them.

Ask yourself, Best always said, just what you would do if you were the villain? He'd tried that. Covered every possibility. But it was no good. He was useless.

His mind began to drift. Trains came and went on the opposite platform, each disgorging rushes of eager, home-bound workers, set against the background of a poster advertising the endless delights of a day out at the Alexandra Palace. Even their numbers began to dwindle.

The lighted disc of the palace's rose window hovered like a new moon on the hill beyond. Marching along below were the line of lamps marking the edges of the south terrace. He must take Betsy and the kids to the palace for a day out – when he had saved enough money.

The answer to the question of what he should do next slid suddenly into Smith's mind like a brightly lit slide at one of the lectures at his uncle's working men's club. It was not heralded by trumpets. Indeed, there was no warning whatsoever. It was just there.

He grinned delightedly to himself. Best always insisted that if you thought hard enough, then had a little rest to give your brain a chance to sort everything out, something useful would pop up of its own accord.

And pop up it had. It was obvious! The Ally Pally! Back where they started.

'We've decided,' announced Littlechild, 'not

to confine ourselves to villains who've shown an interest in literature and poetry. Partly–' he grinned ruefully, looking over the mess of files on his desk – 'because we can't find any except for the poor dead, departed Grimes.'

The inspector was looking less than his usual sprightly self, probably because he was a man of action, and was being coralled. 'So we are concentrating on anyone who seems to be quite educated – that's for the poetry – and who has a reason for resentment against the police.'

'Or thinks he has,' said Best.

'Exactly.'

'A wide brief.'

'And this fellow, being a more intelligent rogue, might keep up with the news,' Littlechild went on firmly. He was clutching two files.

He has the air, thought Best, of someone about to land me with something I'm not going to like.

'We wondered about this one.' He thrust a file at Best. 'It's one of yours.'

Best glanced at the name on the cover: Farley Anderson case? Vaguely familiar. But only vaguely.

'Whitehall civil servant who was embezzling funds?' offered the inspector helpfully.

'Oh, one of those.'

Their proximity to government offices

caused officials to think they could use the Scotland Yard detectives as their own private police – and often did.

'All right. I'll have a look at this on my way,' he said tucking the file under his arm.

'Not sure you should take it out of the office,' said Littlechild, with uncharacteristic timidity. His new Fenian responsibilities must be going to his head.

'Cheadle won't mind,' said Best. 'He's desperate.' Anyway, he thought, the way they're kept here – piled up on desks, on the floor and stairs – anyone could steal them.

'Then, old boy, I'd like to see what you think of this one.' He waved a well-handled blue folder at Best. 'Got a minute for me to run through it?'

He hadn't but Littlechild could be so persuasive in his boyish way.

'Make it quick then.'

'I'll paraphrase it for you.'

Twenty

The ticket clerk at the Alexandra Palace railway station was not being helpful.

He stared at Smith through the window of his little booth and exclaimed, ''Ow would I know if a woman 'ad a lot of luggage?'

'It must be unusual at a station like this,' Smith persisted patiently, 'seeing as how most of your passengers are just here for the day out?'

'No, it ain't,' the clerk muttered petulantly. He leaned forward so that his pockmarked face almost touched the glass. 'We get all sorts. People with hampers, prams and baby carriages. Sometimes even invalid carriages!'

Smith sighed inwardly, recognizing the symptoms of determined non-cooperation with police.

He had hoped that the unlikeliness of someone boarding at the Alexandra Palace station, with trunks and boxes, would quickly prove his supposition right, that this had been the route taken by Alice and Herring on the assumption that police would not expect them to go that way. In his imagination, he had pictured Best being bowled over by his cleverness at recognizing the possibility.

'Well then, isn't it unusual for you to sell many one-way tickets here?'

The ticket clerk straightened up and looked affronted.

Smith was aware that most passengers bought a shilling return ticket to Alexandra Palace from King's Cross, a price which included entrance. Others did board en route at Finsbury Park, Stroud Green, Highgate, Crouch End, Cranley Gardens and Muswell Hill, but they also would want return tickets.

'We 'ave people buying tickets 'ere! Course we do! People who lives round 'ere.'

Smith glanced out over the acres of park to the nearby farmland. Fat lot of locals up there, he thought, and Wood Green residents would use their own railway station, as would the inhabitants of the hamlet of Muswell Hill on the outskirts to the west. But the ticket clerk seemed to imagine that Smith had been suggesting his job was a sinecure.

It probably was, but there was no point in getting officious with the man. He couldn't prove he was being obstructive.

Smith nodded and murmured equably, 'Well, if you think of anything, let me know.'

For a moment the young sergeant had contemplated using a ruse he'd seen Best employ when facing a belligerently unhelpful ironmonger.

'Oh dear, is something wrong?' Best had exclaimed with a concerned expression on his face.

The man had been startled.

'What d'you mean?'

'Well, you seem so, so unhappy. Upset.' The inspector had sought the man's eye. 'A bereavement, perhaps?'

'No, no...' The ironmonger had glanced about confusedly, unable to show his usual recalcitrance in the face of such concern for his well-being.

Best had leaned forward and patted his hand. 'Well, if there is anything we can do...'

After that, the bewildered man had been putty in Best's hands, even managing to assume an almost pleasant expression and regaining a remarkable recall about the matter in hand.

But it was no good. Smith was unable to keep the distaste for the ticket clerk's attitude from his face. He had not, he had to admit, Best's talent to deceive, and probably never would have. 'Extremely honest John', Best called him.

'I'll be with the station master, if you remember anything,' he said, curtly.

Ah, that had the man sitting up. Memory

could be stirred in many different ways, Smith reminded himself.

'I was wrong to blame you for Joseph's death,' Best admitted, quietly.

There, it was said. Now it was done, almost as a means of justifying further consultation with Helen, but he realized how true it was and how sorry he was.

Helen said nothing for a moment, then shrugged and murmured, 'You were heartbroken.'

She was right there. He had been devastated by the death of little Joseph, whom he had lifted from the arms of his drowning grandfather after the sinking of the *Princess Alice* pleasure steamer.

'That was no excuse.'

'You imagined that I just wanted rid of him.'

He nodded ruefully.

'That wasn't true.'

'No.'

Joseph had caught scarlet fever from Helen's nephew after she'd sent him to stay with her sister's family. But he had known that Helen didn't want to keep him. She saw children as a trap for a female painter.

Now, they sat looking glumly at each other, silently remembering.

'The whole thing was all so unbearably sad, Ernest,' Helen said eventually. She leaned forward and patted his hand. 'We can only console ourselves that he was so much happier before he died than he had been since the loss of his family.'

Ever since seeing Helen again at Alexandra Palace, Best had realized how much he had missed her. She was not beautiful like Mary Jane; but, somehow, although worlds apart in background, Helen and he had always felt as though they belonged together, spoke the same language.

'But I expect by now you have a child of your own?' she said, glancing at the ring on his finger.

He shook his head. 'No, not yet. Mary Jane and I are getting married in the spring.' He grinned ruefully. 'We have to save up first.'

'Ah yes, a policeman's pay and a detective's outrageous expensives. Never the twain...'

He nodded. 'I need a few more rewards.'

Rewards were the only thing which helped bridge the gap.

'An Italian girl?'

He shook his head. 'Half-Irish.' He paused. 'She's Joe Collins's daughter.'

'Oh.' Helen was startled. She knitted her brows in puzzlement. 'You do mean that lovely, lively child who was so besotted with you and told everyone she was going to marry you?'

'Yes.' He grinned sheepishly and blushed. 'She's grown up now,' he insisted. 'She's almost nineteen.'

Why did he feel the need to justify himself. Ridiculous.

Helen smiled and clapped her hand to her head. 'I suppose she has. It always comes as a surprise when you haven't seen a child for some time, doesn't it? They grow up!'

She gazed at him thoughtfully. He knew what she must be thinking. Someone nice and uncomplicated after me. Easily moulded – from his own world – would suit him better. In a way she was right. But it wasn't quite so simple really.

'That's wonderful,' she said and smiled again. 'You must let me paint a double portrait as a wedding gift.'

He inclined his head in thanks but thought, how Mary Jane would hate that!

It was strange to be sitting in her cosy parlour once again, but this time warmed only by the fire in the grate. No smouldering glances or passionate kisses.

Almost as though she read his thoughts, she sat up and said in a businesslike manner, 'Right, now what can I do for you, Ernest?'

She laughed suddenly, surprising him.

'That business at the lake! What a triumph for you! Just before the explosion I saw your chief inspector stomping about in a fury looking for you.'

'I know. I was hiding behind some musicians and their instruments,' he admitted.

She chortled out loud in the way he'd never heard another woman laugh.

'Wonderful! Well, you should have seen his face when the bandstand went up. A mixture of astonishment and, yes, relief. Even he must have patted you on the back after that!'

'Nearly,' Best admitted ruefully. 'Almost.'

They both laughed, then stopped and glanced at each other carefully.

'Almost,' she said quietly. 'I can just imagine.'

'He thinks,' Best confided more seriously, 'that you—'

'Being h'artistic,' she put in.

'Being h'artistic, might know where this quote comes from.'

He handed her a copy of the telling phrase.

She perused it for a moment and murmured, ' "News from all nations"? Seems familiar, seems familiar. But...'

'You need time?'

'Yes, and to consult some books.'

'Well, I've got this to read–' he pulled out the file Littlechild had given him – 'if it's all right that I sit here for a while?'

'Of course, my old friend. I'll get Jessie to bring you in some tea.'

Smith was depressed. Nothing was working out as he had hoped. The station master had not recognized the lady in the photograph. Neither had he remembered any such woman being surrounded by trunks the previous evening, although Smith wondered whether he saw much of anything, tucked away in his little office.

Alf Berry, the ticket collector was his white hope, but he remembered nothing either. It turned out that he was new, replacing one recently arrested with others for various fraudulent little ticketing schemes. Alf was too busy, learning the job, to notice what was usual among passengers and what was not.

'We've had a plague of pickpockets on the trains so I've been mostly keeping an eye open for suspicious persons,' he offered helpfully.

Other possible sources of information were the guards who signalled with their flags when their trains were ready to leave then retreated to their luggage vans. If anyone would know, they should, Smith decided. But there were so many of them to track down.

Smith was fast losing faith in his bright idea that Alice had fled via Ally Pally. Besides, it was dark and late and the last trains would be leaving soon.

The young guard, now raising his flag to wave away the train presently getting up steam, had been eager to assist, which was a change. Indeed, he had been overcome with excitement with the very idea of talking to a Scotland Yard detective. But he hadn't known anything.

All Smith's effort had been for nothing. He'd spent a lot of money on cabs getting here. He'd have to fight to get it back – particularly if his quest was in vain.

And there was another night away from Betsy and the kids in prospect. Maybe she was right. He should become a private detective like some of the others had done. More money and less worry.

What to do next? Smith wandered disconsolately into the now empty waiting room. At least it was more sheltered there than on the draughty platform, and even warmed a little by the gas jets. Why it should be this cold on an August evening, he didn't know. Maybe he was tired. He knew that he ought to trek back to Wood Green, and on foot to save money, but didn't know where he was going to find the energy, never mind the will.

The door creaked and the first passengers for the next train began to enter. He avoided their eyes, not wishing to become involved in polite chat. Someone sat beside him and began clearing their throat. Drat.

'Excuse me,' said a young and nervous voice.

Best looked up reluctantly. It was Alf Berry, the trainee ticket collector.

'About them trunks.'

Smith sat up. 'Yes?'

'Well, I *do* remember some. But they weren't with a lady. Well, not the ones I saw. They was with a man.'

'A one-eyed man?' exclaimed Smith, slapping the surprised young fellow on the back.

The lad's eyes widened. 'Yes! 'Ow did you know that?'

'Ah,' said Smith with a broad and relieved smile, 'has nobody told you that Scotland Yard detectives know everything?'

Twenty-One

'Hallo young Smith! You look happy!'

The exclamation caused Smith to pause in his headlong rush back up the stairs into Alexandra Palace. Coming down the stairs, now almost level with him, was Mr Coxwell, the famous aeronaut.

In truth, Smith would rather have continued his dash to the telegraph room. He wanted the Yard to know what was going on.

But Coxwell had been kind to him, not to mention lending him the money to get the train back to the palace after his involuntary balloon flight.

The two men stopped and exchanged greetings, Smith explaining that he had just had a wonderful lead in an investigation and was anxious to pass on the news to his colleagues.

'Well, I mustn't hold up the law,' laughed Coxwell.

'Look,' said Smith, blushing, 'I haven't forgotten the money you loaned me. I've put in a docket to the receiver to claim it back and—'

'Oh, don't be silly, my lad. There's no hurry. Look, why don't I come along with you – we can talk as we go. There's a favour I want to ask.' He registered Smith's anxious glance. 'Don't worry, I can walk fast, too.' He smiled. 'It was fortuitous bumping into you. We're both in luck today.'

Smith hurtled back down the stairs towards the station after he left Coxwell, where the nine thirty evening train was about to leave for King's Cross from Alexandra Palace station.

The guard, a stocky, dignified man with an upright stance and a stiff neck, was just completing the downswing of his green flag to indicate to the driver that all carriage doors were closed and he could therefore commence the journey.

He retreated into his van and was reaching for the door to close it when he saw the tall and handome young man speeding recklessly in his direction. He put out his arm to ward him off but as he ran Smith pulled out his warrant. He held it before him and called, 'Police, urgent business,' and fell into the carriage knocking the guard over as he did so.

The train had already started to move so Smith pulled the door shut behind him before reaching down to help the indignant man to his feet.

'How *dare* you...'

'Sorry, sir!' Smith panted. 'Vital Scotland Yard matter.' He brushed the man's previously pristine uniform jacket and said, 'In fact, you are the very man I wish to consult.'

'Me?'

'Yes, I'll just get my breath back then I'll explain.'

Well, that worked. The guard was sufficiently puzzled and distracted to forget the indignity. The man from the Yard wished to consult with him. I've learned something else from Best, Smith thought.

'Oh, no, it was a lady what was with the trunks,' the guard insisted. 'A middle-aged lady.' He paused. 'A fellow did help her and the porter on with them, but I reckoned he was just being polite.' He shrugged. ' 'Cos he went off when I took over, so that's what I reckoned.'

'Did he have one eye?'

'Didn't get a good look at him, sorry.' He pulled back his shoulders importantly. 'Too busy seeing the trunks stowed right and attendin' to my other duties such as the safety of the passengers.' He shook his head. 'Tell you what, though, I have to admit I thought it a bit peculiar, a mighty bit peculiar, in fact, for a person to be leaving from this station with all that stuff.'

Smith nodded attentively.

'I means, look at it like this. If you lives at Wood Green or Bowes Park and wants to go to King's Cross, you've got Wood Green or Bowes stations. If you wants to go east, or down to the City, then there's Palace Gates, and if it's one of those posh houses in Muswell Hill you're going from, well then, there's Muswell Hill station, isn't there? And that's one stop nearer where you're going to so it would be daft to come 'ere.'

'And she was going to?' asked Smith, trying to suppress his impatience. Once 'consulted' there was no stopping the man.

'I was just coming to that, wasn't I,' the guard said a little huffily. The train trundled to a halt at Muswell Hill and he jumped out to fulfill his platform duties.

When he reboarded, flag-waving done,

212

Smith became almost obsequious. 'You've been extremely helpful,' he said as the door shut once again. 'You were saying, she got out at...?'

'Well, that's another funny thing. You would have thought, wouldn't you, with all that luggage, that it would have been King's Cross? If you was going somewhere nearer on this route, well, you might as well get a cart from home to take you there.'

Smith held his clenched fists down by his sides and kept the eagerly attentive smile on his face. 'But, it was in fact,' he put in, 'somewhere nearer?'

It obviously was, but at this rate the man might not tell him in time for him to jump off the train to make enquiries at that station.

'Yes, it was.' The guard shook his head in wonderment. The train was slowing down again.

'You wouldn't guess how many stops she went?' He shook his head and grinned knowingly. 'Unbelievable!'

Smith's smile was crumbling and the urge to strangle the man became overwhelming.

The train had stopped. The guard was about to alight. Smith grasped his sleeve. 'How many stops!' he pleaded. 'It's important!'

'Two, only two,' said the little man as he stepped on to the platform of Highgate station.

The guard quickly became hidden behind disembarking passengers.

Smith dodged between them shouting, 'That means *here*? She got off *here*?'

But if the little railway servant heard, he gave no sign before stepping back on board, leaning out and raising his green flag once more.

'Here?' yelled Smith again.

He was bringing his flag down fast. 'Course,' he grinned smugly. 'Course. Thought you would have worked that out. You being a smart detective an' all.'

A beautifully designed circular fell from the Dubois file – another case he'd been advised to research for possible enemies – as he opened it, reminding Best what an unusual case it had been.

Three men, Wood, an Englishman, and Frenchmen Dubois and Arbre, had placed advertisements in foreign newspapers, announcing a forthcoming London exhibition of works by Continental artists.

They had also sent the aforesaid beautiful circulars, designed by Wood, who was himself an artist, to many of the leading European painters suggesting that they submit works.

The artists responded in droves. Any doubts were quickly allayed by the receipt from the Exhibition Executive Committee, thanking them for their splendid exhibits and assuring them they would be kept informed of progress regarding dates and venue.

One might imagine that rewards in this type of ruse were small. But many of the newly wealthy, middle classes had grand, new houses with large expanses of wall in need of adornment. The same people had portfolios in need of filling with etchings and watercolours, for guests to admire when relaxing after dinner with a glass of port. Therefore, the market for quality art was thriving and, of course, if you could buy quality more cheaply...

It wasn't until some time later, when details of the exhibition arrangements had failed to emerge, that Scotland Yard began receiving complaints.

Inspector Maurice Moser and Best, when a sergeant, had been put on the case, or handed the docket as police parlance had it.

Not surprisingly, they found that the birds had flown from the addresses given, so they attacked the problem in a more oblique fashion. They perused the Yard's list of receivers of stolen goods. From this, they selected the names of those who handled choice paintings – then put a couple of the most likely suspects under surveillance.

One of these, Bertie Lidell, was known to

Moser who caught him with a couple of very nice watercolours under his arm.

Thinking to save himself, Lidell ratted on his suppliers: Dubois, Arbre and Wood. Eventually, all four went to prison and most of the paintings were retrieved, which raised the status of Scotland Yard no end in artistic circles.

Lidell had not completed his prison sentence. He had an accident, contracted that dangerous infection, erysipelas, and had died. Dubois, Arbre and Wood did their time and were duly released.

Moser had scribbled a note on the bottom of the file:

Saw Dubois playing a cornet in a street near Charing Cross. Said he was saving money to go to America. Arbre has gone back to France. Wood fallen on hard times and is very bitter because his wife died while he was locked up. Dubois said, 'If he sees you, he will kill you.'

Well, there was your bitterness against the police. Of course, most criminals were bitter about being caught. But the fraudsters had included a couple of romantic quotes on their circular about 'the glory and the good of art' by Robert Browning, and Shakespeare's 'Look here upon this picture'. So there were your rhymesters.

There was also their playfulness in calling themselves Wood and (in French) 'of the wood' and 'tree'. The artists defrauded could be said to have come 'from all nations'. Well, at least most of the European ones.

Better see if he could find Wood.

'Yeh, I remember her,' exclaimed the driver of a four-wheeled cab.

The queue of vehicles left at the cab rank at Highgate Station had been short. But, wonder of wonders, the driver of the third in line, a well-kept growler with a black horse whose shiny flanks glinted under the street lamp, had proved to be the one he sought.

'Remember where I took her to, as well,' said the chirpy, grinning driver before Smith even had time to ask. 'Want to go?'

Smith nodded eagerly. 'Yes, please.' He certainly did, and there was no question that this expense would be claimable – if his quest was successful. He jumped up on the box to sit alongside the driver.

'Did she know where she was going?' he asked, as the cabbie gave a little tug on his reins and made a soft, clicking signal to his horse.

'How d'you mean, sir?'

'Did she ask you for a suitable place to go or did she give you an address.'

'Oh, gave me an address.' He guided his horse out on to busy Muswell Hill Road. 'Knew where it was, too.'

Ah, so Maud and Alice had not been entirely alone in London, after all.

Twenty-Two

'It's by William Cowper,' said Helen, as she entered the room with a leather-bound book under her arm. 'From "The Winter Evening" which is book four of his poem *The Task*.'

'You found it! Cheadle will be pleased.'

Helen glanced heavenwards. 'This is to please you, not that dreadful man.'

They both laughed.

She wants to please me, he thought.

She laid the volume on a bookrest and opened it where she had placed a leather marker. 'Cowper was an early nature poet. A little bit mad but he wrote some wonderful verse and several hymns, "God moves in mysterious ways", and all that.'

Best had heard of Cowper, vaguely. But, as a Roman Catholic, doubted that he was familiar with the hymns. That had been another problem between them.

218

'Listen to this,' Helen said. 'It's from verse four of "The Winter Evening". She began reading in her soft, low voice:

" 'He comes, the herald of a noisy world,
With spatter'd boots, strapp'd waist, and frozen locks;
News from all nations lumb'ring at his back." '

'Hm.' Best wrinkled his brow. 'Read it again, please, will you?'
She did.
'I don't quite understand. Who is this "herald" who comes? Is it winter?'
'Yes, I think it must be. It goes on:

"True to his charge, the close-pack'd load behind, Yet careless what he brings, his one concern
Is to conduct it to the destin'd inn:
And, having dropp'd th' expected bag, pass on.
He whistles as he goes, light-hearted wretch,
Cold and yet cheerful: messenger of grief."

'Hm, maybe not. Maybe it's meant to be the outside world. The verse goes on with things you read about in newspapers: the fall of stock, births, marriages and death.

And here's a bit which could be pertinent:

"Is India free? and does she wear her plum'd And jewell'd turban with a smile of peace, Or do we grind her still? The grand debate, The popular harangue..."

'India,' he mused. 'Well, it is involved in the Afghan war, of course. And that was one of the possibilities we came up with, apart from the Irish troubles.'

'Could Quicksilver be an Indian – or a mutiny sympathizer – wanting India to be free?'

Best sighed. 'That's something to keep in mind, I suppose, to look at closer. We'll do that – and warn India House.'

As he had suspected, discovering the context actually illuminated little, confused things more.

'It does seem,' said Helen, reading his thoughts, 'apart from the India possibility, that the context is immaterial. Maybe we only need to take the phrase on face value.' She paused. 'Is there some international event taking place in London?'

'Not that we know of. We've been wracking our brains and thumbing through newspapers but haven't been able to pinpoint anything.'

They contemplated the matter for a moment.

'So, could it be something to do with an international organization?'

Best shrugged. 'We think that's another possibility but–' he spread his hands – 'it's such a wide canvas.'

'Well, even if you haven't found the answer, we've at least blocked off one side alley and come up with a small lead.'

'Thanks to you,' he smiled. He knew she was trying to stop him becoming pessimistic. She had remembered that his spirits tended to be either way up or low down.

He knew he should hurry back to the Yard but it was very peaceful and relaxing sitting here. The heavy scent from the bowl of Old English roses on the table by the window, mingled with that of the hot scones on the plate she now proffered.

'As good as Mrs Briggs's?' he asked as he took one.

They smiled quietly at each other, enjoying the shared remembrance.

Helen wiped her hands and went back to the book. 'This bit is evocative,' she said, 'and ties in with the messenger being the outside world the writer wants to shut out.'

She began reading again:

' "Now stir the fire, and close the shutters fast,
Let fall the curtains, wheel the sofa round,

And, while the bubbling and loud-hissing urn
Throws up a steamy column, and the cups,
That cheer but not inebriate, wait on each,
So let us welcome peaceful ev'ning in." '

She glanced out of the window at the gathering dusk, smiled serenely, and closed the book.

Why did I let her go, he thought.

The Cowper poem was endless, and not easy to comprehend at a glance, so Helen promised to give it further attention when she was alone again. She would also try to tease out any clues hidden in its dense depths.

Meanwhile, they fell to discussing the other possible routes to the unmasking of Quicksilver, among them the Dubois case.

Helen sat up at the mention of Wood. 'Eric Wood?'

Best checked back in the file. 'Yes.'

'I know him.'

'I was hoping you might,' said Best, 'but as he is so down on his luck I thought he probably wasn't painting any more.'

She shook her head. 'You're right. People won't trust him after that business. He looks like a scarecrow now,' she admitted sadly. 'Not that that's a bad thing for him.'

'What do you mean?' said Best raising his eyebrows in surprise. She had never really been a hard-hearted woman. A determined one, yes. It had taken him some time to discern the difference.

'Well, he has to be thin for the posing he's doing for Bertrand.'

Bertrand was a relative of Helen's and a very successful painter.

'He's in great need of gaunt men just now,' she smiled, putting her head on one side. 'He's doing a series on the Etruscan wars, so he needs some starving prisoners. He's also painting a huge panorama of the poor of London streets, so he wants gaunt beggars for that. Unfortunately, his best model has passed on. He had consumption.'

'I wouldn't have thought it hard to find starving men in this city.'

'It isn't – but they must have the stamina to pose and the understanding of what it's about. It's more difficult, you know, if you are very thin. Your bones get sore. Also–' she shrugged – 'if they are very desperate they will steal from the studio, and the other rooms if they get the chance.'

'I didn't know Bertrand painted pictures of the destitute.'

'Well, he's no Gustave Doré,' Helen smiled. 'But I think Mr Fildes and Mr von Herkomer have awakened his conscience.'

Luke Fildes and Hubert von Herkomer's

depictions of the suffering poor, hoping for admission to a workhouse, had touched many hearts – and several pockets.

'Don't look at me so cynically, Ernest. You know he's a nice man with a family to keep.'

She was right there, he supposed.

'Trouble is Marie's so kind to Eric, keeps feeding him up. Bertrand says if she goes on like that she'll do the man out of a job. He'll be too plump for a starving beggar or a slave.'

'I *must* see him,' said Best.

She nodded. 'Very well. Meet me at Bertrand's studio tomorrow morning at nine. I expect Eric Wood will be there.'

'He mustn't know who I am.'

'All right,' she smiled. 'We'll dress you up as a Praetorian guard, or some such.'

Twenty-Three

'We're full up,' declared the round-cheeked, round-bodied little woman who answered the door. Her accent was familiar. Just like Alice's.

When Smith failed to turn away, the woman stepped back to get a full view of this tall young man. 'Bit late to be lookin' for lodgings, isn't it?'

'I'm not,' Smith replied.

'What then, man?'

'I'm looking for – Alice.' He'd nearly said Maud.

'Sorry hin. She's gone.'

'Oh, blow!' He looked so tired and crest-fallen as he leaned against the door jamb that she softened and allowed him into the hall.

'Are you a friend, then?' she asked.

'Sort of...' He held out his hand. 'I'm John George.'

'Mabel,' she replied extending hers. 'Well, her stays were short, I must say. She came here late last night and left the very first

225

thing this morning.' She led him into her parlour.

'Have you been friends for long?' asked Smith as he sank gratefully into one of her plump armchairs.

'We was in the same children's home. A long time ago mind, that was.'

'Wykham's?'

'Aha. That's right.' She glanced at him in surprise. 'Did *she* tell you about that then?'

'She did. Not a nice place, she reckoned.'

'No.' Mabel paused. 'She doesn't usually talk about it. She had an even worse time than me.'

'Do you know where she's gone now?'

She shook her head. 'She wouldn't say. Very peculiar. She didn't seem like herself at all.'

'I have to see her. It's urgent.'

'Did she not tell you where she was going either, then?' Her currant-bun eyes grew wary.

'No,' he sighed. He thought, Hurry up and distract the woman. She's getting suspicious and if you give her too long to ruminate...

'Can I see the room she slept in?'

Mabel was taken aback. 'Oh, I don't know about...'

'She said she would let me know, you see,' he explained. 'She might have left a message there for me or something.' He knew it sounded lame.

'If she'd left *any* message it would have been with *me*,' Mabel said firmly and she began to rise from her chair.

'There might be a train timetable there or some other clue,' he explained.

'Clue?' There was an icy silence. 'What do you mean, "clue"?'

Oh dear. Bad choice of words. Tiredness catching up on him.

'I'm worried about her, you see.'

'I think,' said Mabel, fully erect now, 'that Alice can take care of herself. Always has done.'

He'd shot his bolt. She began moving towards the parlour door and clearly expected him to do the same.

'Usually, I'd agree.' He shook his head sadly. 'But she must have been so upset by Maud's sudden death that...'

'Maud's death!' The woman was clearly astonished. She sat down again. 'What are you talking about, man?'

She hadn't heard. Ah, that was a bit of luck. He recognized the possibility of a trade-off. Bad news was first rate currency.

Smith launched quickly into the sad and oh-so-dramatic tale of death on the roundabout. In the process, Mabel somehow got the impression that he was a concerned neighbour and friend.

After such shared melodrama, Mabel could scarcely refuse to allow Smith to see

Alice's room. Indeed appeared happy to do so in the hope, Smith guessed, of gleaning new and more terrible titbits.

It transpired the room had not yet been re-let.

'I hadn't cleaned it up and didn't want the bother of taking on another guest tonight. That's why I said I was full,' Mabel explained as she pointed the way upstairs.

Mabel puffed and blew as her little legs pulled her plump form up the steep stairs. Were all northern women short? Smith wondered. She paused on the first landing to get her breath.

'It's all been a great shock, I suppose,' she said putting her head back to look up at Smith. 'But I can't see why Alice should be so upset. That woman didn't treat her right. There she was, saying that they were like a couple of sisters. Well, if you treated your own kin like that – worked them to death and kept them poor...'

'So, why didn't she leave?'

He knew the answer before Mabel replied. The master's hold over the servant. 'Because that bitch said that if she did, after all she'd done for her, that she wouldn't give her a character.'

A domestic without a character was as good as in the workhouse.

'And you know, hinny, even I've got to admit, that Alice is a plain lady. Never taken any man's eye. Not that she ever had the chance...'

She halted on the second landing and looked up at Smith again. 'Good riddance to that Maud. I'd have done the old bat in, if I'd been Alice.' She leaned forward and opened the door to room three.

'Was there anyone with Alice when she arrived?' asked Smith as he glanced around the modest room where she had slept.

'No. Who would there be, hinny?'

'Oh. Nobody. Just wondered.'

There was no revealing timetable or impressions of handwriting left to investigate. Only a couple of pink and white glass ornaments on the dressing table.

'A cabbie did help her up with her luggage. I couldn't believe it – you know what they're like.'

'All the way up to this room?' Smith asked as he opened and closed the dresser drawers. They were empty save for their floral paper lining.

She nodded. 'Aha. I think so, anyway.'

'But you saw him leave?'

'No. Well, I was too busy talking to Alice. I was so taken aback to see her. It's been such a long time and...'

Smith had moved over to the battered mahogany chest of drawers. 'So he could even have stayed the night?'

Mabel's eyes widened, then she laughed.

'Oh, I don't think so, hinny!'

Smith said nothing.

She knitted her brows disbelievingly. 'You're not telling me our Alice had a fancy man?'

'Not sure. Maybe.'

'Well, you're full of surprising notions, young man. Tell you what, though, hinny. If she did, she never said anything to me – and he didn't come down to breakfast neither!'

At the same moment their eyes lit on the cigarette ends which had been ground into the ashtray on the bedside table.

'Did this cabbie have one eye by any chance?'

Mabel pursed her lips and her own little eyes grew more pensive. 'Aha, hinny,' she admitted eventually. 'Yes he did.'

Smith moved on to inspect the light-oak wardrobe wedged into the corner of the room to the right of the window. He turned the key and pulled the knob. Nothing happened. The door stayed shut.

He put his left hand on the frame and pulled again, harder. As he did so the wardrobe began to rock, then the top tilted forward as if some heavy weight was throwing it out of balance. Had some of Alice's baggage proved too cumbersome and been left behind?

The wardrobe began to topple. Smith put his hand out to catch it. As he did so, the door sprang open and the heavy object fell out. It left them in no doubt why the cabbie had not come down to breakfast.

Arthur Herring was clearly very dead. There were massive wounds to the front of his head, inflicted, it seemed, by the heavy brass candlestick which lay beside him on the floor of the wardrobe. The blood around his wounds was dark and dry. He had obviously been dead some time.

But wasn't it odd, thought Smith, after a hysterical Mabel had been escorted down-stairs by a skivvy, that there were no blood-stains anywhere else in the room? The man would scarcely have gone into the wardrobe voluntarily so that his assailant didn't have a messy room to cope with? Maybe he was hiding in there at the time he was attacked?

Smith pondered the matter for a moment before leaning forward to pull back the bed-clothes.

The pillows and sheets told their grisly tale. They were crusted with blood – also long since dried and darkened. Arthur had been lying down when attacked. May even have been asleep.

There were no stains on the bedhead or the wall above. That was odd. Even odder, the wallpaper at that spot looked lighter than that which surrounded it, although there had been an effort to shade off the edges of the paler circle.

Alice must have used some of her hard-won cleaning skills to wash away the blood splashes. With all her experience she would know that one must use cold water to dissolve the blood, not hot, which congealed.

Best replaced the sheet, went downstairs, wrote a note and sent the now gawping skivvy off to get the local constable.

Then he set about calming Mabel so that he could extract some more information from her. But even when settled down to quiet sniffling, every now and then Mabel would throw back her head and howl, 'I divn't believe it! She was like a sister to me! I divn't believe it!'

Smith cut into one of these outbursts by demanding, 'Who came to collect Alice this morning?'

'Nobody. Nobody,' Mabel insisted between sniffles.

'So her trunks are still here?'

'Oh, no,' she shook her head. 'Of course not. She got a growler!'

'Whose cab? Someone you use regularly?'

'No. No. She wouldn't hear of that, I didn't know why.'

I do, thought Smith.

'So, she'd arranged for one to pick her up?'

'No, no.' Mabel shook her head. 'She just

went out and got one herself. Insisted on just picking one up off the street. It's not that difficult around here.'

Clever woman, thought Smith. Now, how can I trace that? The cab could come from anywhere for miles around.

Smith contemplated the first in the stretch of railway termini which were strung out along the north side of the Euston Road. Remarkable buildings, all three.

The workmanlike King's Cross was built of pale yellow-ochre London brick and, despite the central clock tower, resembled a toy fort. It was the terminus of the Great Northern Railway where Alice could have completed her journey from Alexandra Palace.

Why hadn't she? Why hadn't she stayed on the train and taken the opportunity of a quick getaway to Doncaster, York, Newcastle or Edinburgh? Probably because she knew they'd expect that. So it was unlikely she'd gone there today. He'd leave King's Cross until last then.

When the first find-the-cab line of enquiry dried up, Smith had decided to move on to the next logical step – investigating the nearest main-line railway stations.

Of course, Alice might have travelled only a short distance on a local line, or had the cab she'd summoned take her to the East

End, where she could lose herself in the endless warrens of seedy streets. She may even have crossed London to Victoria station and boarded a train heading for the Continent – as so many fugitives did. In which case, she'd probably be in Paris by now.

The local policeman had been none too pleased when Smith had greeted him, described briefly the reasons why cab driver, Arthur Herring, had landed up dead in a wardrobe on his patch, then dashed away, promising to telegraph the divisional headquarters and Scotland Yard from King's Cross police station.

Help and further information would arrive from the Yard soon, he promised. He wasn't sure that it would at this hour. They'd probably all gone home by now but he felt that time was of the essence in his pursuit of Alice.

'You can only do what you think is right at the time,' Best was always telling him. Fine, if you turned out to be correct, he had once admitted, but if you turned out to be wrong...

Smith pushed such demoralising thoughts from his mind. He'd try St Pancras first. That marvel of red-brick, high Gothic, fairy-tale pinnacles, towers and gables was home to the Midland Railway. She might have fled to Birmingham from there.

Britain's bustling, industrial, second city would be just the place to hide from the world.

Detective Sergeant John George Smith sat on a rather superior bench in Euston station's vestibule, the magnificent Great Hall. It was a place which usually delighted him with its deeply coffered ceilings and double sweep of white marble stairs, punctuated at the foot by a huge statue of the railway king, George Stephenson.

But John George was tired, despondent at his lack of success so far – and very hungry. The fairy-tale St Pancras station had not supplied him with a happy ending. Far from it. None of its servants admitted to ever having clapped eyes on Alice and her trunks, while pointing out that they were highly unlikely to remember her from among the passing throng. Had she been a pretty young woman, the story might well have been different.

John George had realized that it was not sensible to continue his task without something in his stomach, so he bought a pork pie and a jar of ale from one of the street stalls. Much cheaper than the station buffet.

He began to devour the pie, holding his left hand beneath to catch any crumbs, stopping every now and then for a swig of the ale. That was better.

But there was little he could do about his tiredness until his self-appointed task was done. He closed his eyes to rest them, just for a moment, to refresh them. A short pause would help him reassess his plans and let his food go down...

He fell asleep instantly.

The last trains of the day arrived and departed and the stream of travellers, their friends, relatives and servants, petered out. John George slumbered on.

Since he looked reasonably respectable, if a little rumpled, the beadle did not seek to have him removed. He was obviously a passenger who had missed his last train and who would be moving on with the dawn departures.

Twenty-Four

The rumbling noise, at first distant, grew steadily closer. Suddenly, a horse and cart was speeding towards him.

Oh God, he must get out of the way!

But he couldn't move. His feet seemed stuck. He was just making a final, desperate effort to escape when, somewhere, a whistle shrieked.

Smith's eyes shot open, then snapped shut again, blinded by the strong morning light. Squinting and blinking, he forced them open again, pulled himself up into a sitting position and gazed around bewildered. Where *was* he?

Slowly it all came back: grand staircase, beautiful marble floors, statue. Good grief, of course, he was in the Great Hall of Euston railway station! Realization set in as he sat there, head in hands, trying to come to terms with the situation. Eventually, he lifted his head and glanced blearily at the hall clock. A quarter past five. Oh God! He was really done for now.

The hall was empty, save for a lone porter

trundling and rumbling his iron-wheeled luggage chariot across the wide concourse – the horse and cart of his nightmare.

A weary young couple, dragging three reluctant children, came through the south entrance, then two workmen who hurried by without a glance, their hobnailed footsteps clattering and ringing on the marble floor.

How was he going to explain this? He'd sped from the murder scene, to the displeasure of the local police, when perhaps he should have remained. All because he'd got an idea in his head. Some whim, some ridiculous certainty that he needed to keep on the trail of Alice before it faded away and she disappeared beyond reach. Then what had he done? Fallen asleep with the job half done, that's what.

His mouth tasted foul, his bones ached, he felt seedy and unwashed but, most of all, sick to his stomach in the certain knowledge that his career, his whole life, was tumbling down around him.

No more being a detective. Probably no more being a policeman after he'd been dragged up to answer a charge of dereliction of duty. What could he do instead? He was trained for nothing else and now he would have no character either.

He tried to fathom how Best would have handled this situation. The inspector had always advised him, that if he was caught out in some petty infringement, he should admit to what he was obviously guilty of but think of another, better reason why he had done the deed. Learn from the villains, in fact. Caught with their hands in the till they'd be 'Just returning some money. They gave me too much change, guv'nor'.

Trouble was, Smith could think of no good reason for going to sleep on a bench in a railway terminus while on urgent duty – only the real one which was that he had been exhausted. But he knew that wouldn't do. He felt he'd let Best down twice over.

More rumbling from two more luggage barrows trundling by. He watched dazedly, realizing that he was only putting off the moment when he would have to take action; hand himself over, confess his sins and begin the end of his present life.

Well, he thought defiantly, that could wait until he'd pulled himself together a little. Might as well do the deed in as dignified a manner as possible. Besides, he wanted a pee first.

The scene grew a little livelier. A small rush of hurrying passengers and a porter, trying to get speed up, but thwarted by the heaviness of his load. Maybe he could do something like that. Become a luggage porter. He sighed, at least he was fit and strong. But wouldn't he need a character, even for that?

Trailing behind the overloaded barrow was a small woman with abundant flaxen hair drawn back into fashionable, sweeping, dove-like wings.

She must be going a long way, Smith thought idly, to necessitate such an early start with so much luggage. Probably catching a connection to Fishguard and maybe on to Dublin, or going up to the Scottish Isles via Glasgow. All places which Smith had never seen, and was unlikely to now that he would no longer have the chance to go on escort duty, collecting or delivering prisoners and suspects.

The young woman did not seem overjoyed with her privileged life. She was keeping her head down and her eyes averted. Perhaps she imagined he was one of those white slave traffickers?

No, she's a bit too old for that, he realized as his eyes followed her now retreating form, despite the impression given by the hair. There was a staidness about her gait, and her carriage was not erect and lively enough.

He stared disbelievingly. There was something very familiar about the figure, now hurrying through the archway.

Smith leaped to his feet and began to run as though his life depended on it.

Once through the arch he could see no

sign of her. Had she gone to the ladies' rest room? For refreshment? Or was she already on a train?

He kept running, glancing feverishly along each platform, hoping for a glimpse of her or the luggage. Suddenly, he spotted the trunks being loaded into the guards' van at the far end of an express which was belching start-up steam. There was no sign of the woman.

The indicator board said: Departure time five twenty. Two minutes away!

He flashed his warrant at the ticket collector and yelled, 'Police. The woman with the trunks – which carriage?'

'First class. Number seven, I think,' the man shouted after him.

As Smith sped along the platform, clouds of steam billowed from the engine as it puffed up a warning of imminent departure. The ceremony of the closing of the carriage doors had begun. Not many, since there were few passengers.

Breathless with exertion, Smith leaped on to the step of number seven first class carriage, shouting to a startled guard in passing, 'Police! Stop the train!'

Smith burst in, just as the woman was reaching up to place her small red carpet bag on the overhead rack. He laid a restraining hand on her other arm and panted into her startled face, 'Alice Harper, I am arresting you on suspicion of murdering Arthur Herring and Maud Forrest.'

'Where are you going now?' asked Mary Jane, glancing at his best waistcoat. 'Somewhere special?'

'Oh, no,' he shrugged.

'Where, then?'

He hesitated. He had avoided mentioning that he had bumped into Helen at the Alexandra Palace and now it had become too difficult to explain his further contact with her even though it had been quite innocent and accidental. In any case, why upset her unnecessarily?

But he couldn't bring himself to tell her an outright lie.

'I'm going to be an artist's model,' he grinned, inviting her to share the joke. 'Posing for a painter!'

The look on her face told him that he should have thought up a more general truth, such as 'I'm going to interview a suspect', which he was. Had he not been in such a hurry, he might have.

'With that Helen,' she burst out, hurt in her eyes. 'I knew you were seeing her again. I just *knew*.'

'No, I'm not,' he insisted. He tried to grasp her hand but she pulled it away and began to look tearful.

'It's work. I bumped into her on this en-

242

quiry quite by accident and she knows one of the Quicksilver suspects – and he is going to model for Bertrand today – so she just arranged...' He spread his hands wide. 'She just arranged for me to be there too.'

He grabbed his jacket. The tears were starting.

'Look,' he said, sighing, 'if this model is Quicksilver, we can close this case and I'll be home much more. Isn't that what you want?'

He tried to kiss her goodbye but she turned her head away. He sighed with exasperation and left thinking, I'm too old for her. Later he was to wish he had tried harder.

'Wood's here,' Helen assured Best, as she opened the door of Jacques Bertrand's icing-sugar mansion in Holland Park.

That was good. Not a wasted journey then.

Bertrand was still at the family breakfast table. He jumped up at the sight of Best.

'Ernest! How good to see you after all this time.' He perused him head to foot. 'Still as smart as paint and up to the minute in fashion,' he commented, with obvious delight.

It was this directness, plus his sleekness and the way his tendency to touch, as he was doing now to Best's arm as he shook his hand, that had put Best off at first. That, and the suspicion that Bertrand and Helen were on over-intimate terms for mere friend.

It transpired that Bertrand was, in fact, a devoted family man (apart from the odd dalliance with one of his models), who kept a fatherly eye on Helen and her sister after they had lost their parents. He also helped Helen obtain commissions.

That, and the terrible times Bertrand and Best had gone through together, when the girls were endangered in the canal murder case, had made them into brothers.

Best declined the offer of a cup of coffee in favour of getting started. His guise, it was decided, would not be as a fellow model, which would be too time-consuming in preparation and, perhaps, too deceitful.

Instead, he would be a pupil painter and assistant, before an easel set up alongside the master. Best had dabbled a little when undercover on the baby farming case in Islington, so at least knew how to pretend to be an artist.

Bertrand's other assistants had set up the scene: Wood begging, gaunt hand outstretched beside a waiflike young woman holding a flower basket, both lit overhead by a street lamp.

The stench of oil and turpentine began to make Best feel quite sick and a bit giddy. He should have had some breakfast before he had dashed out this morning. Fortunately, the first break came sooner than expected; Bertrand, with a wink, pleading shoulder problems.

Marie brought in tea and sandwiches, so Best sat alongside Wood to eat his. Helen got into conversation with the girl by asking whether she might be available to pose as an invalid for a forthcoming picture.

At first, he and Wood merely munched gratefully and companionably, but as the edge of their hunger abated they fell into idle chat about the weather, the studio and painting.

Wood's voice was surprisingly strong, but his bony hands shook and he shivered a little now and then, despite the warmth of the studio.

Best confessed to finding it difficult to make a living as a painter. To his surprise Wood laughed, before patting his hand in case he was offended.

'I know the problem only too well, old man,' he said. 'I'm a painter too, you know?'

Best said he didn't.

'Well, I was, and I got a bit desperate and decided to do something about it – but it all went wrong in the end.'

Best was an expert winkler-out of secrets so it was not long before the full tale of Wood's clever wheeze saw light of day.

'It worked, too,' he exclaimed with some pride.

245

Best said he thought it an inspired idea, which was true.

Wood nodded his acknowledgement.

'You wouldn't believe how many paintings we received.' His pale face grew quite pink with pleasure at the memory. 'But then,' he shrugged, 'the bluebottles got wind and it all went wrong.'

Further probing revealed that Wood was, indeed, bitter about his prison experiences, feeling that the severity of the sentence outweighed the seriousness of the crime.

'These were all wealthy men, after all. Successful painters. Could afford to give a few away.'

He certainly harboured some hatred of police, whom he thought could have treated it all more lightly.

'I'd bet you'd like to get back at them?' Best exclaimed sympathetically.

Wood thought about it, then shrugged. 'Did at first, I suppose. Was consumed with the idea. Then, when I was right at the bottom, starving on the street after I got out, this copper gave me one of his sandwiches and some of his brew he'd heated up on top of the street lamp, like they do.'

He took a swig of his tea as if in memory, before reaching for a fourth sandwich. Best could see what Helen meant about him eating himself out of a job by filling out those hollow eyes and gaunt cheeks.

Wood ate quickly and looked about him nervously as he did so, as though fearful someone might snatch the food away.

'This copper,' he said, suddenly pausing and using his ham and lettuce sandwich as a pointer to his words, 'told me I was too young to go down the drain. He got me into St Luke's workhouse so I could pull myself together. Then Mr Bertrand came around looking for thin models. So you see, I owe something to the police after all. Well, at least one policeman.'

It could all have been a tall tale. The man might have guessed he was a policeman. But somehow Best didn't think so. He decided that Eric Wood, of Wood, Dubois and Arbre, was not Quicksilver after all.

But he had been wrong before.

Twenty-Five

'I didn't mean to kill her,' Alice said, wearily.

Smith stared at her across the interview room table.

'You put cyanide in her capsules and you didn't mean to kill her?'

She nodded. 'Aye, man, I was really mad when I did that,' she explained. 'She treated me rotten over them potatoes, spoke to me like I was dirt!' For a moment, anger sparked in her tired eyes.

'What potatoes?'

'The ones I'd just got in.'

Smith sighed. 'From where?'

'The garden, of course. Just because she didn't like the look of the potatoes we had in the rack, she sent me out in the rain to dig up some more. I got all muddy and soaking, then she went and threw out the ones I'd dug up. Said they were blighted.' Her eyes were wet now and deeply sad. 'But they weren't. Not really.'

Smith sat forward with a puzzled expression on his youthful face. 'But there isn't a vegetable patch at Chilton House.'

'I know that, man! This was up in New-castle, wasn't it?'

'Oh.' He paused, feeling his way. 'So you filled her capsules with cyanide when you lived up north, but you didn't use them when you were there?' He hesitated, frowning, perplexed. 'Did you try to?'

'Oh no. Of course not!' she exclaimed, as though this was another silly question he should have known the answer to. He was beginning to feel some sympathy for Maud. 'I never *meant* to kill her at all, you see. Not really.'

Smith didn't see. In fact he was totally bewildered.

He hadn't wanted her to talk at all, just yet. They were still in the railway police office at Euston and he'd rather she'd waited until they were back at Wood Green, where she would be charged. But she had taken no notice of his requests to wait, so he had been obliged to give her a caution, pull out his notebook and write down as much as he could.

Once she'd recovered from the initial shock of capture, Alice had become quite calm, showing no fear. Seemed almost relieved, in fact. A not uncommon reaction. Trying to keep one step ahead of the law could be a weary and lonely business.

'She'd been so nasty about it,' Alice explained, 'I thought to myself, I'll show you,

you bitch. There was some cyanide in the garden shed for killing rats so I went and got it and pinched some of her capsules and put it in.'

'But you didn't intend to poison her?' asked Smith, disbelievingly.

She looked at him with a sad half-smile on her face. 'Oh, no. Honestly, hinny. I just felt better after doing that – knowing that I could kill her if I wanted to.'

'But you kept them. Just in case.'

'Well, no. Not deliberately for that, man.' She sought for the right words. 'It was just that they were there and when I got mad at her I would take them out and look at them and feel better for knowing I could kill her, if I wanted to.'

Smith, who was loved by his family and enjoyed the friendship and camaraderie of his colleagues, tried to imagine how it would feel to be like this woman. No relative to care about her and no friend to confide in.

'But you told us that people said you were like sisters,' he broke in. 'They couldn't always tell who was the servant.'

'Oh we were – in a way. But, believe me, I always knew who was the skivvy!' Smouldering resentment accentuated the rising Tyneside inflexion. 'She never let me forget that, did she?

'Mistresses always think you're close, like

sisters – when it suits them. When they want company. But you've always got to be nice all the time whether you want to or not. They don't.'

'You could have left.'

'Oh, no, I couldn't, hinny.' She looked down at her smart moire dress, probably the nicest she had ever worn, and smoothed and patted it absently. 'I'd nowhere else to go, had I? I had no money of my own, she saw to that, and she'd not give me a character if I went.'

She sat up a little more proudly. 'I did try once, you know. But she set the polis on me. Said I'd stolen money from her. But I'd only taken what was due.'

'But you *did* poison her in the end, didn't you?' Smith reminded her, with a trace of exasperation.

Alice put her head on one side and gave him a rueful half-smile. 'I know, hinny. I know.'

There was something almost childlike about the admission.

'Why?'

'She found out that I'd been selling some of the groceries to Arthur.'

Smith raised his eyebrows.

'I had to!' she exclaimed. 'I had these terrible painful piles and I needed some money to buy ointment but she wouldn't give me any. She kept me so short.' She

251

paused, then burst forth once more: 'Said why did I *need* pocket money when she kept me and paid for everything?'

'So you put the tablets in her pill box?'

'Oh, no. It wasn't just for that. No...' She became thoughtful and a blush began creeping up her worn cheeks. 'It was because of Arthur.'

'He told you to?' Ah, so she was going to blame him. He was dead so couldn't deny it.

'Oh, no. What it was, you see, was that he asked me out, and I thought my straw hat was too shabby and wanted to buy a new one. But she wouldn't let me have an advance. She just laughed and said it was all vanity.' Alice stopped, remembering.

She took a deep breath. 'It was then I put the poisoned tablets in. I got so angry thinking as how I'd had no life of my own and this was my only chance – with Arthur.' Her face was crumpling now and her voice cracking.

'Almost right away I wished I hadn't.' She twisted her hands agitatedly, reliving the crisis. 'I tried to get them back, but she came in the bathroom and I had to pretend I was looking for something else. After that, I kept watching her to see if she was about to take one. I was going to knock them out of her hand and pretend it was an accident.

'But then,' her voice grew quieter, 'we went up to that palace place. She wanted to go on the roundabout. There wasn't room left for me but she wouldn't wait. She sent me to get some ice cream – even though that meant I would lose my place in the queue.'

She stared out of the police office window on to the busy platform where people were hurrying for their trains, anxious, but free.

'When I came back, she was dead.'

'You saw her, then?'

'Aye, hinny. I did. I knew what must have happened, so I ran away.' She sighed heavily. 'Then I thought that would look suspicious. So I came back.'

Tears began spilling down her thin cheeks.

'I miss her, you know,' she said.

Smith shook his head in wonderment.

'I do,' she assured him. 'Well, she was all I had, wasn't she?' She smiled tremulously. 'And sometimes we *were* like sisters.'

Smith nodded slowly, before saying quietly, 'What about Arthur?'

There was a long silence, during which Alice refused to meet his eye. Eventually, she mumbled, 'He tried to blackmail me.'

She was crumbling now, tears in her throat, on her face and dripping on to her smart, moire dress. 'He wasn't much, but I thought he liked me.'

She was unable to use the word love, probably because she'd never had any.

'He was lying in bed at Mabel's when he said how much money he wanted. Just about the lot – and that his wife was coming to meet him. When I said, what about us, he laughed and said he'd never look at a stringy old maid like me.'

Tears were choking her now. Smith leaned forward and handed her one of his large, checked handkerchiefs which had been lovingly laundered by his Betsy. She grasped it, but did not use it – just sobbed and sobbed with uncontrollable grief.

'It was all too much for her,' said Smith. 'She had the candlestick in her hand and this fury overcame her and she just smashed it down on his head.'

'She knows she'll hang,' said Cheadle. It was more a statement than a question.

Smith nodded sadly. 'I don't think she cares.'

'An 'oo can blame 'er,' said Cheadle with uncharacteristic sympathy. He paused, then said, 'You did well, lad, pulling Mr Best's irons out of the fire for 'im.' He nodded towards the inspector.

'Oh, both of us were fooled by her,' Smith insisted.

'Yes, but it was 'im that was in charge, weren't it?' He glared at Best. 'And 'im that's got all the h'experience and is *so* clever.'

'Do you think,' asked Smith, eager to change the subject, 'when all that about how badly Maud treated her, and the blackmail, that the judge might take pity on her? Mabel says she'll speak for her.'

Cheadle shook his head. 'If 't'd been just the one, lad, mebbe. But *two*–' he sucked his teeth – 'can't see it.'

'What *I* can't see,' said Best afterwards, 'is how you knew that Alice would be leaving at dawn on that train.'

'It was a hunch,' said Smith airily. 'You always said I should follow my hunches and...'

Best gave him an oblique glance and sighed. 'John George, you disappoint me. You're *blushing.*'

'No, I'm not,' the younger man insisted, as the pink glow crept up his neck.

Best shook his head. 'Will I never make a fibber out of you?'

'Well, what it was,' said Smith, 'I think Mabel mentioned something about Alice having a friend in Birmingham.'

'That's better,' said Best. 'But a bit more definite – leave out the "I think".'

'Funny Cheadle didn't ask what I was doing there.'

'That's because you got her. He doesn't care how. That's what it's all about, John George. He doesn't want to know that you were having a kip on a waiting room bench when the lady tries to outsmart us by coming through *after* we've made our enquiries there.'

'I *wasn't* asleep in the waiting room,' Smith said indignantly.

Best raised his eyebrows enquiringly. 'Oh?'

'I was in the Great Hall.'

Best clasped his sides and let out a bellow of laughter. 'Oh, very discreet, very discreet. You should have put out flags!'

Quicksilver had gone quiet. They had not heard from him for six weeks. No bombs had gone off at the headquarters of international organizations or newspaper offices during that time. Williamson had returned from his holidays, so the responsibility no longer hung so heavily over Shore and Cheadle.

'Don't know whether we should just be relieved, or be holding our breaths,' said Best.

'He might have died,' said Smith, hopefully.

'Or be locked up somewhere.'

They exchanged doubtful glances.

It was the usually optimistic Smith who voiced the mutual feeling: 'But, I don't really think so, do you?'

'No.'

Twenty-Six

The weather was acting very strangely. One minute the day was bright, warm and still, then the sky darkened abruptly. A spiteful, gusty wind blew up followed by a spattering of large raindrops which turned quickly into a torrential downpour. Just as suddenly, the rain ceased, the skies cleared and the summery sunshine returned. Soon, the cycle began again.

'For heaven's sake,' exclaimed Best irritably, glaring at the sky, 'it's not April – it's the beginning of October!'

He resented the distraction of the ever-changing weather, of having to duck into doorways to avoid a drenching, which would sully the pristine nap of his new, high-crown bowler.

He had other things to think about. Such as the Chancel case he'd had to shelve when Quicksilver began his antics, plus the reason for his current expedition. This was the curious matter of the disappearance of Lady Barncliffe's diamonds from her padlocked luggage en route between Windsor and

Paddington railway stations. Then there was Helen. Mostly, there was Helen.

Indeed, since he'd first glimpsed her, bent over her drawings in the reading room of the Alexandra Palace, she had scarcely been out of his thoughts. Oddly, he kept reliving the mad dash to the Triple Lakes and imagining what it would have been like had he not got there in time. The thought was unbearable.

He was also feeling guilty about not feeling guilty enough about his being so preoccupied with another woman, when his marriage to Mary Jane was looming.

But it tore his heart that she had looked so sad the last time he had seen her. How had she known that Helen was in the picture again?

However, the image in his head, as he stepped blithely off the Praed Street pavement, was of Helen and the way they had giggled childishly together when they had been shushed by the old boy in the reading room.

A deafening male shout: 'Look out! Look out!' and a high-pitched female scream tore through his reverie. He looked up to see a manically speeding hansom cab bearing down on him. The driver leaning forward, whip flaying, horse at a frantic gallop, head up, mane flying.

Best was so transfixed by the sight that the horse was on him before he could react. At the same moment, he felt himself being yanked backwards by his coat tails and collar. The cab raced by within an inch of his nose, and his immaculate jet-black bowler tumbled forward under its wheels.

As the saving hands released him, Best toppled into the filthy gutter, stunned by the suddenness of it all.

'You ought to be more careful, mate!' shouted the burly station porter who had saved him and who was now stooping to help him to his feet.

'*He* ought to be more careful!' exclaimed his middle-aged lady passenger. Her purple brocade bosom was heaving and her matching hat feathers were alive with indignation. 'What about that ruffian?' She jabbed her umbrella after the disappearing cab. 'He didn't even slow down – quite the reverse! Quite the reverse!'

She stopped still, turned and looked thoughtfully at Best before saying, 'For all the world it seemed deliberate.' She frowned and enquired politely, 'Is someone trying to kill you, young man?'

Best straightened up, glanced ruefully at the crushed pancake that had been his bowler, and admitted, 'I'm certainly beginning to think so, madam.'

Indeed, this was the third incident in the last few days which had threatened his life. His assumption, that the other two had been accidents, was now in question.

The first involved a window box falling from a second floor Whitehall office, smashing inches ahead of Best and spraying soil and plant detritus all over his gleaming, Derby lace-ups.

The cause, as the concerned office manager and beadle had explained, was that the metal strut holding the box had rusted, worn thin and snapped – just as Best happened to be strolling by. A regrettable accident for which someone would answer for their negligent inspection.

The second 'accident' had occurred at Farringdon Street underground station, as a train had belched its noisy, smoky way alongside the platform.

Best was certain that, as the train approached, he had felt an almighty shove in the small of his back. Again, other hands had reached out to save him and, on the crowded platform, he'd been unable to identify the pusher. Indeed, all those around him had seemed only concerned for his welfare, so he had put the incident down to over-eager jockeying for position.

But these incidents now assumed a more sinister aspect. There had certainly been nothing accidental about that vision from hell he'd seen bearing down on him in Praed Street. The driver had been as purposeful as it was possible to be. But who could want me dead? Best wondered. The fleeting glimpse he had got of the cabby gave him no clue.

'You must inform the police, instantly,' the purple-bosomed lady insisted, while eyeing him with some suspicion. Clearly, she was wondering what he might have been up to, to deserve such retribution. Was he, despite his smartness, just another ruffian?

'I will, madam, I will,' he assured her gravely.

He did too. He told Cheadle.

To his surprise the old boy took the matter quite seriously.

'We're a bit short of bilingual detectives since the Turf Frauds,' Littlechild pointed out sanguinely, before adding, 'it would reflect badly on old Cheasy if he allowed one of them to come to a grisly end.'

Smith tendered a more down-to-earth view of the chief inspector's uncharacteristic concern.

'Mum likes you. You got them together. She'd be unhappy if you joined the angels, as she puts it.'

'Ah. Might be some cutting off of the old steak and kidney pie?'

Smith nodded. 'Probably. Plum duff, as well,' he grinned. 'Too big a price.'

'What I can't understand,' Best had said to Cheadle, 'is not only why and who wants to kill me, but how he knows where I'm going to be?'

'Hmph. That's simple,' said the chief inspector, emphasizing his words by repeatedly thrusting his sausage-like forefinger at Best. 'Either 'e's shadowing you all the time or, more likely...' He paused, sighed, then said with great seriousness, ''e's one of us.'

A stunned silence greeted this pronouncement. It was not one Cheadle would make lightly. He hated bent coppers.

He pulled thoughtfully at the thinning ends of his greying moustaches and enquired, 'This 'ere h'enquiry at Paddington station – lead to much, did it?'

Best stared at him, then shook his head slowly. 'Nobody there knew anything about it.'

'Right. False call. Like what I said. It's one of us.'

Once they had realized that someone was out to end Best's life, they decided that, apart from checking up on detective office security at the Yard (a joke, if Best had ever heard one), there was little they could do short of keeping him in the office. But he would have to come out sometime. In any case, that wouldn't make much sense if his enemy *was* an insider.

Cheadle did keep Best in for a while, however. Two hours, to be exact. He made Best sit alone in the inspector's room and instructed him to think about which colleagues he had most offended during his service. The very words 'which' and 'most' intimating unsubtly that he expected a long list.

Twice, the old boy popped his head around the door with further advice. One was to say, 'Don't just think about the big broils. If the bloke's a nutter, 'e could 'ave been set off by some little barney.'

The second time was to advise Best not to limit his list to colleagues of similar rank. 'Could be someone higher up. You might have done something to make 'im look bad – or not done something you should 'ave.'

Despite Cheadle's allusions, he got on well with most of his colleagues – once they'd got over him being a bit flash and foreign-looking. And that didn't apply so much in the Yard's Detective Branch as many of the others were second generation immigrants.

As for mistakes that would upset senior officers, well, of course there were some, but none which leapt instantly to mind as being likely to put their career in jeopardy.

'Don't worry,' said Cheadle, glancing at his meagre list. 'Now you've started stirring the pudding, you'll find a plump raisin or two popping to the surface of its own accord.' That was quite poetic for Cheadle. Clearly there was promise of spotted dick on the menu tonight.

So Best was let out while his raisins

plumped up – but never alone. Always, he must take a second pair of eyes along. Mostly, Smith's.

At the moment, Smith's head had no room for raisins – it was full of aerial balloons.

Mr Coxwell had lived up to his promise to take the Smith family aloft, and this had turned out to be quite the most exciting event of their lives.

What's more, the famous aeronaut had roped in Smith as one of his groundsmen for an extraordinary contest. Eight aerial balloons took off at the same time from eight different points on London's outskirts, including Crystal Palace in the south and Alexandra Palace in the north. The idea had been to see how far each balloon could travel during the ninety minutes after take-off.

Smith's chatter was liberally laced with how they had poulticed valves and the vagaries of air displacement and the weight of the various gases per cubic foot.

Best had never known the young man so garrulous and enthusiastic, and let him prattle on over their ordinary in the Rising Sun pub, which sat in the entrance to Great Scotland Yard. He was describing the pre-parations for another forthcoming contest, when Best pulled out his watch and pointed to Smith's half-consumed pint and half-eaten mutton chop.

While Smith took the hint, Best seized the opportunity to say, 'John George, I need your help.'

The younger man blushed guiltily over his last forkful as he remembered the threat to Best, swallowed and said quickly, 'Anything. Anything.'

'As you know, I've got to recall which officers I've offended during my service.'

'Nobody I know of,' exclaimed Smith loyally.

Best inclined his head. 'Come on.'

'Well, not enough to want to kill you,' Smith grinned.

'Doesn't have to be,' said Best. 'If he's off his head, it could just be a little thing.'

'Like with Quicksilver?'

'Right.'

'Could it be Quicksilver?'

Best shrugged, 'Possible. But if so, why has there been no hint of it before? Seems to be a different vendetta, somehow.'

'Yeh. I suppose.'

'Anyway, while I'm sending my mind way back to plump up some raisins, if you could start thinking about the jobs I've been on with you. The Canal explosion and the murder of Nella and the *Princess Alice* business.'

'You got up Cheadle's nose with that one,' Smith chuckled, 'making him have a post mortem.'

'He might be pleased to get his own back by having one on me!'

Smith didn't laugh at that. He couldn't help recalling how he had felt when he had thought that Best was one of the victims of the *Princess Alice* disaster. This man, who had given him his chance and who was like a father to him, only more so.

Smith couldn't bear the thought of Best dead. He gulped the last dregs of his ale and repeated, 'Anything.'

Twenty-Seven

The final letter arrived on the morning of Tuesday 19th October, the day after Alice was hanged.

It said:

So here we go for the big one.
You'd better give it your Best this time.
Ha Ha!
Ill news hath wings, and with the wind doth go.
With love from Aggy.
QUICKSILVER

'What in God's name does that mean?' groaned Cheadle, shaking his head with irritation.

'Well, it answers one question,' said Chief Superintendent Williamson. 'It seems that Quicksilver, and the person who has been trying to kill Ernest, are definitely one and the same.'

'Hmph!' said Cheadle. 'Just as I thought.'

'Who is Aggy?' Williamson asked.

'No idea, sir,' shrugged Best. 'Don't know anyone of that name.'

'Give it some thought,' advised Williamson. Then he smiled slightly and observed, 'She's obviously no beauty or you would have remembered!'

The inspectors and chief inspectors gathered around his desk exchanged manly grins and winks.

'Yes, sir.'

The chief was keeping it light, but Best was in no doubt how seriously he took the matter. They hadn't seen Williamson's lighter side since the Turf Fraud Scandal, two years ago. Hardly surprising that he seemed less trusting, since half his department had landed up in prison for fraud. He was looking older, too, but he was still a handsome, kindly-looking man, with his squarish face and a neatly-trimmed beard. The satin trim on his black jacket gleamed and was set off, as usual, with a rose

267

buttonhole from his own garden.

'How are you getting on with that long list of those you've offended?'

Again, a slight twinkle to show his appreciation of the strain Best must be under. He certainly felt a lot more pressure now it was suspected that he had caused this whole thing – unknowingly or not.

'I do have a few, sir.' He pulled a piece of paper out of his jacket pocket and handed it to the chief. It listed five names.

'They were all a bit trivial – just the usual sort of upset with a colleague – and all soon forgotten. Apart from Armitage, that is. That was different all right.'

'Oh?'

'Yes. I caught him stealing from a jeweller's shop in Upper Street.'

'Ah. This sounds more promising. Explain.'

Best told about that ghastly time. An honest policeman's worst nightmare. Nowhere near as bad as that time with The Toff, of course, but nasty just the same.

Best had been on his way home in the middle of the night having been kept late on a job, when he had suddenly spotted a man standing very close to a jeweller's window. At first, he thought he might just be looking at some of the contents lit by the street lamp. But when Best got closer he realized what the man was doing.

He was cleverly hooking out rings and necklaces with a stick which he had pushed through a gap in the metal grill and a hole in the window beyond. The man had suddenly become aware of Best's approach, looked up, then fled.

But Best had been young and fit and had caught him, only to discover he was Constable Armitage from the opposite shift.

It had been a sickening moment which he hated to remember. He also hated to remember the man sobbing and begging to be let go. Pouring out a tale of woe about debts which were no fault of his own, as he did so.

'Was he keen on poetry?'

'Not that I know of, sir. But I only knew him by sight and I can't remember anything like that to do with the case.' He paused. 'He did swear revenge, though. Said he would see to me if it was the last thing he did.'

'Oh, well, that does look promising.'

'I was about to see if I could track down those on the list.'

'No, no.' Williamson held up his well-manicured hand. 'We'll put someone else on that. You just give your mind to poor, plain Aggy and whether it was her husband or father you offended so mightily.'

'Yes, sir.'

'Anyone familiar with this couplet? "Ill

news hath wings, and with the wind doth go"?'

A shaking of heads all round.

'It has me beaten.' He looked across at Littlechild. 'You follow this up, John, and the rest of you consult those books you've got left over from your education exams. I'll ask my wife, she's a poetry enthusiast and I'll put Mr Vincent and his erudite friends on to it.'

'Helen Franks might be able to 'elp an' all,' Cheadle broke in, clearly not happy with the idea of Mr Vincent beating them to it. 'She did last time. She has books she looks in.'

Best suppressed a small smile. Helen would be amused at being given a testimonial by the old ogre himself.

'Is that so?' said Williamson. 'Well, we need all the help we can get. Send for her.'

Best nearly choked. It was obvious Williamson had never met Helen. Cheadle had, though.

'Er. I'll leave that to Ernest,' he said, bestowing Best with an unusually benevolent smile. ' 'E's 'er friend.'

'Fine. All done?'

It was.

He pointed at Best, a serious expression creeping into his eyes. 'Thinking cap on, Inspector.'

'Yes, sir.'

Best applied his mind as well as he could, but it kept drifting back to Alice. He'd been to see her just before she'd gone to the gallows. In fact he and Smith had made several visits since her conviction and sentence.

They had found her sad, but serene.

'It's not as if I'm giving up much, is it?' she'd pointed out.

Sadly, they had to agree. On that occasion she had seemed more concerned with the state of Holloway prison's laundry cupboards which she had been busy sorting out. 'Just you wait,' she had said, 'as soon as I've gone they'll let them go to hell again.'

That was something else they noticed, she'd begun to swear a lot since being sentenced to death. Maybe she had always wanted to, but daren't.

Now and then her mind had strayed to what might have been and to Maud. 'I still miss the old cow, you know, hinny. She wasn't that bad, really.'

Both men had kissed her goodbye. As soon as they had done it they realized it was a mistake. Up to then, as she prepared for death, she had borne up and even joked with them.

But the show of affection had almost undone her. Her mouth had trembled and tears started into her eyes. But she had fought them back, straightened up and declared, 'I'm going to a better place.'

Best couldn't disagree with that.

Suddenly she had wailed, 'I will be forgiven, won't I?'

The padre, whose job was to comfort her, hesitated but Best had broken in with a firm, 'Yes, of course. I'm certain of it,' and she had been calmed, shook their hands and had gone.

And that was it.

Best clapped his hands to his head. Oh, God, and that was it, too.

The Toff grinning and saying, 'He's gone to a better place', then laughing. But how could it be! It was impossible!

It had not been some small slight or disagreement with a colleague after all. It had been something terrible. The worst thing that had happened to Best in his service, apart from the death of his young wife, Emma.

Now, it all rushed back in on him in a dreadful wave, and he held his hands over his ears as though to drive out the words 'He's gone to a better place', and the laugh...

Williamson and Cheadle stared at him.

'Why didn't you think of this before?' exclaimed Williamson angrily.

'Well, at first it just didn't occur to me. I was looking for someone I'd offended and in any case I thought it just couldn't be – he was transported for life. Went out on the last shipment to Western Australia.'

Williamson sighed. 'Well, it seems that somehow this "toff" has got back.'

'Could it be a relative of his getting their own back?' offered Cheadle.

'Maybe. They would have to care about him a good deal though, wouldn't they, and he doesn't seem very lovable?'

'Might have left them destitute,' persisted the pragmatic Cheadle.

'If they were, doubt if they would have the energy for all this,' the equally pragmatic Williamson pointed out. He looked at Best, 'Tell me about him. Why "The Toff"?'

'He spoke posh. Been to public school – was from a good family who lost everything – it was said. But he was bitter. Thought he should have come in at the superintendent level or straight into the Detective Branch. He hid his anger most of the time, but now and then, usually when he was in drink, it would burst out. His proper name was Rutter, Algernon Rutter.'

'Hmm. I wonder why he didn't come into the Branch. They were doing direct entry then, as well, weren't they?'

This was a sore point. Following the Turf Fraud Scandal, Howard Vincent had re-introduced direct entry by higher calibre applicants. He and the Home Office were convinced that better class folk were the solution to most problems, ignoring the fact that the previous experiment had mostly been a disaster.

'Had the languages for the Branch, I think. But there were rumours about him being a bit shady and that he'd been given the benefit of the doubt over some transgression.'

'Oh, well. We had one lucky escape.'

'Don't know how true it was – you know what this job's like for gossip. Anyway, he said he would get there just the same, under his own steam.'

Williamson raised his eyes to heaven. 'Well, at least we know who we are looking for,' he said. 'That's a step forward.' He sighed.

He was looking worn, thought Best.

'You know,' Williamson went on, 'this man is going to do something terrible. We desperately need to know where and when.' He mused, almost to himself, ' "News from all nations".'

Smith put his head around the door and announced that Helen Franks was downstairs and was asking for Best.

Best frowned. 'But I haven't asked her to come. Not yet.'

Smith shrugged. 'She's saying she must see you, it's urgent. Something about the newspaper.'

'Bring her up,' said Williamson. 'We need

all the help we can get.'

'Yes, sir.' Smith hesitated and looked from Cheadle to Williamson. 'Sir, is it still all right for me to have tomorrow off?'

The senior men exchanged doubtful glances.

'I did promise Mr Coxwell,' he added anxiously. 'It's the International Aeronautical competition and...'

'The *what*?' exclaimed Williamson, holding up his hand.

The three men stared at each other, stunned.

'The International Aeronautical competit...' began Smith when he realized it was a question which didn't require an answer.

'Of course,' said Williamson.

'There's reporters from all over the world,' put in Smith, 'and...' His voice petered out.

' "Ill news hath wings",', murmured Best, ' "and with the wind doth blow...".'

At that moment Helen arrived looking pink, irritated at being kept waiting, and waving a copy of *The Times*. 'This race,' she said, without preamble. 'It seems to me with all the international interest...'

'News from all nations...' nodded Best. 'We've just realized.'

'It's a bit tenuous, but...'

'No, no,' said Williamson, who had stood up as she entered. 'We've had another letter which talks of wings and the wind blowing.

We think that ties it up,' he explained. 'Do take a seat, Miss Franks. I'm sure we could still use your help. You were ahead of us.'

She sat on one of the office chairs opposite and looked around at their worried faces. 'You know who it is?'

Best nodded. 'We think so – and it's not good news.'

For a few seconds they all sat lost in contemplation, as if it were necessary to allow everything to sink in before deciding what to do.

'I should have thought...' Smith exclaimed suddenly, his face reddening. 'I mean, I knew and...'

Williamson waved him silent.

'We all knew. We all should have thought. It's been in the papers long enough.'

They all nodded and looked rueful.

'But now we know – and what's more, we are lucky to have the services of an expert like yourself who will now educate us to exactly what will happen–' he spread his hands wide – 'officially, that is...'

Smith looked startled. 'Not exactly an expert, sir...'

'Compared with us, you are. Tell us everything you know about the event.'

Smith looked at Best who nodded as he said, 'From the beginning. Assume we know nothing.'

He straightened up. 'Right.' He cleared his

throat, took a deep breath and began: 'Right. As you know, it happens tomorrow...'

'You know this man, Rutter,' Cheadle said to Best. 'What's he like?' he demanded. 'What's he going to *do*?'

Best had shaken his head for the tenth time and muttered, 'I don't know!' Ever since he'd realized who Quicksilver was, the vision of Algernon Rutter (a sight he had worked so hard to forget) had begun to come into focus. But the image had not yet fully crystallized. Cheadle's hectoring did not help.

'Give him time to think, Arthur,' Williamson said, laying a hand on Cheadle's arm. 'It takes time.'

'We ain't got no time,' Cheadle grumbled but less belligerently. He was fond of Williamson. Had known his father, one of the first superintendents, back in the old days.

'Go over that description again,' Williamson urged quietly.

'Tall, black hair and short, hard beard and moustache. Well, at least he had then...'

'These fashions ... these stupid fashions,' Cheadle raged. 'Thought up by cons, if you ask me – so we can't h'identify them no more.'

Best had already told them that the shape of Rutter's face, noted as 'thin' on his file in the convicts registration office, was not quite right. More shaped than that implied. 'He had high cheekbones and hollow cheeks – oh, and a loose kind of mouth,' said Best, 'with a line down the side. Yes, that's it, lines down the side.' He drew semicircles around his own cheeks. 'And he didn't exactly lisp, but sounded his esses into a sort of "sh".'

There was a short silence while they absorbed this information and Best raked his memory.

'Penetrating dark eyes – they were the most noticeable thing – always casting around, seeing they didn't miss anything ... Oh, and he could run. Run like the wind. They called him Mercury on Division because he was as swift and cunning and...'

He stopped and slapped his forehead, 'Mercury! Mercury! Oh, what a bloody fool I am!'

Williamson nodded. 'Another name for quicksilver. Don't blame yourself, Ernest. It was a long time ago. The poetry, any idea about that?'

Best grimaced, still smarting at his own stupidity. He shook his head. 'No.' He tried to think. 'Not unless...? No, it couldn't be that.'

'What?'

'Well, the others used to tease me because I bought poetry books, but they were for

Emma, when she was sick.'

Williamson nodded. 'He was taunting you.'

'His walk. His walk.' Cheadle exclaimed, having had enough of airy-fairy supposition. 'Was it like it says 'ere?' He banged the file. 'Upright?'

Cheadle was a great believer in identification by a man's carriage and walk, and it exasperated him that younger detectives didn't value the knowledge more. 'You can spot 'em at a distance, get a bead on 'em from far back,' he always insisted.

Best nodded slowly. 'Yes. Yes, I think so.'

'For God's sake, man!'

'I'm trying,' exclaimed Best. 'Give me a chance!' He closed his eyes.

Cheadle didn't say anything, just pushed himself up in his seat and stared crossly out of the office window into Great Scotland Yard.

'Not really upright,' said Best eventually. 'Held his shoulders straight and his head up in a superior sort of manner but his whole body leaned forward. Tilted and, yes–' he waved his hand in the air excitedly as though trying to pull knowledge out of the ether – 'that's it. That's it! And, like I said, he was always looking about him, side to side, like this.'

Best imitated the man's twisting and turning of the head as he walked.

He had done it so he could see what he could get into next, Best later realized. Who he could threaten with arrest, or do some violence to on the excuse that they had resisted arrest.

At the time, Best had only seen Rutter as a hard but successful officer with a slightly superior manner, always catching villains and breaking up fights; had even looked up to him.

Now, he knew better. Could spot the signs earlier. Officers who were always breaking up fights and being assaulted could be the very persons who caused all the trouble in the first place.

'Under all the supposedly aristocratic bearing, he was belligerent,' sighed Best, 'bloody belligerent.' Then, bitterly: 'On the take, corrupt. A bully.' He closed his eyes to blot Rutter out. 'A vile man. He was a vile man.'

If that were all. If only that were all.

Twenty-Eight

For the second day running Best glanced around him, shook his head and shivered. 'I don't believe it – snow! It's not even November yet!'

'As long as those blasted things take off today, that's all I care about,' snapped Cheadle.

Yesterday had been a fiasco. They had arrived in the morning to find the balloon ascent had been postponed. The unexpected overnight fall of snow had caught everyone unawares, making it impossible to inflate the balloons in time. The keen north wind hadn't helped.

'Well, at least the postponement has cut down the crowd,' Best muttered, as he glanced around the oddly ethereal scene.

The snow was still lying quite thickly and the sky remained dark and heavy with the promise of more. Occasional shafts of sunlight did manage to break through the stratified layers of cloud, glancing off the tiered wall of the magnificent structure above them.

With its long, low, stepped layers, the Crystal Palace sometimes looked like nothing so much as an oblong wedding cake, glittering curved transepts standing in for the usual arbour.

It truly was the most amazing building in Britain. Even more amazing was the way it had been dismantled, after serving its initial purpose of housing the 1851 Great Exhibition in Hyde Park, to be reassembled here, on a hill in Sydenham in South London.

Pockets of mist had gathered in the hollow below the North Water Tower where, deflated, like child's toy balloons, were the two huge aeronautical wonders. This time, despite appearances, they were all ready to be inflated for flight.

The French balloon, at a capacity of 42,000 cubic feet, was much the larger, while the British, Eclipse, could only guzzle a mere 28,000 cubic feet of gas.

All had been evened up by the weight of the passengers and instruments carried by the larger French balloon. With this apparatus for gauging the temperature at high altitude, it was hoped that some insight might be gained into the cause of the persistent London fogs.

It was these loads which were presently preoccupying Best.

Ever since yesterday's moment of truth,

the detectives had been frantically exercising their minds as to what nasty surprise Quicksilver might have in store for them.

Would he make one of the balloons explode over the crowd? Cause the French balloon to disintegrate, thereby causing a dreadful diplomatic incident? Or set fire to the Crystal Palace?

At one time, people had imagined the glass and iron palace could not burn, but there had been a fire which destroyed one wing, so they had all become somewhat nervous at yesterday evening's fireworks by Mr Brock, which had gone ahead as planned.

'Bring it down with an explosion, more like.'

'All that flying glass,' Smith had shuddered. 'People would be cut to ribbons.'

Explosions were on everyone's minds at the moment. Only last month, a mysterious package of dynamite had been found tucked under a railway sleeper on the London & North Western line, between Bushey and Watford. The fact that who planted this 'bomb' and why, was a complete mystery, added somehow to the apprehension. This had come in useful as an excuse for the police vigilance at the balloon event.

'Can't see there's any relation myself,' said Williamson. 'The railway bomber is more likely to have something to do with the rent riots in Ireland, but people aren't to know that, thank goodness.'

From this distance, the spectators who gathered around the deflated balloons resembled sprinkles of soot around huge, multicoloured boiled sweets.

A greater density of sooty particles fussed around the business end of the crafts. According to Smith, who had been appointed their resident authority on the subject, these were groundsmen poulticing the valves, an exercise which prevented the gas, about to be injected, from seeping away.

Gas tubes had been inserted in the openings, ready for the filling up, and the cars were about to be affixed. Smith was disappointed that he was not able to help but had been smartly advised that only he and his new friend, veteran aeronaut Mr Coxwell, stood between a successful outcome and a terrible calamity.

'That,' Mr Coxwell informed Best, pointing to the man now overseeing the attachment of the car to the Eclipse, 'is our competitor, Mr Thomas Wright. He has taken over from me as the official Crystal Palace balloonist.

'The man taking the photographs is Mr William Cobb, photographer to the Royal Military Academy at Woolwich. I can't tell you the name of the man with the notebook, but he is a literary gentleman connected with the Central Press Association.

'They are the crew and passengers of the British balloon.'

He paused before continuing: 'Those three men–' he pointed to a group deep in conversation around the valve – 'are Mr Adams and Mr Whelan, aeronauts from Manchester, and Mr Jackson from Derby. Of course,' he went on, 'both contestants have checked their assistants in case a stranger should attempt to muscle in...' He smiled. 'As they would in any event. Tampering has been known.'

None of them looked the least bit like Rutter, but he might be employing someone else to do his dirty work. It had been cold then, as well, but not snowing. Best had been wearing the heavy uniform overcoat which brought even fit young men almost to their knees with weariness before the night was up.

Strangely, despite its bulk, which impeded you if you had to run, the garment wasn't all that warm. How did the police outfitters managed that trick, they would wonder? Material which was thick, heavy as a cartload of coal, but not warm?

Rutter had been waiting for him outside the Methodist Chapel, on the corner of Barford Street and the Liverpool Road where their beats met up.

Rutter didn't look cold, but then he kept

warm in one of his many bolt holes. His step was light and his head, as always, was swivelling. He grinned at the frozen Best. 'Been trying too many door handles, old man?'

'Just doing my job,' Best replied, feeling foolish.

Rutter gave a shout of laughter which sent an alcoholic wave towards Best. His helmet, Best noticed, was tilted at a jaunty angle.

'What we need tonight is a swig of something stronger,' he said as Best began to turn into the side entrance to the Royal Agricultural Hall – the Aggy – towards the night-watchman's room.

'No, not for me,' said Best. He drew the line at alcohol on duty. 'You go ... I'll...'

Best had seen too many officers brought down by booze. In any case, he wanted to be a detective and did not want to blot his copybook for the sake of a quick nip of the hard stuff.

Rutter scowled, then spotted the new advertising notices for the Christmas Fair opening the following day.

'No,' he shrugged, then grinned. 'I'll come with you first.'

Mr Coxwell had turned his attention to the French crew.

'That is M'sieur De Fonvielle, the aeronaut and the president of their Academie,' he said, indicating a bewhiskered, middle-aged man who looked more like a worried bank manager than an adventurer among the clouds with a gigantic balloon for a chariot.

One side of the balloon was now lifting as the gas began flowing in. The artist, standing back, furiously sketching the moment, was M'sieur Perron, the French Academie vice-president, Mr Coxwell explained, while the third passenger, checking the mooring ropes, was Englishman, Commander Cheyne R.N.

Ah, that was him. He was famous for his proposed Arctic expedition by linked balloons to the North Pole. An insane scheme which had so excited Smith that, for a while, Best was afraid he was going to volunteer for that suicidal mission.

Coxwell turned his head sharply. 'I'm afraid I do not know that young woman.' He pointed to an approaching figure wearing a snug chestnut brown coat, a matching astrakhan hat and a tentative smile.

'Don't worry,' said Best. 'I do!'

He strode over to her, his boots squelching through the snow. 'Mary Jane, what are you doing here?'

'I brought your scarf and gloves.' She blushed and held them out towards him. 'You forgot them and it is so cold today.'

He looked fondly at her, hoping his

irritation wasn't too obvious. 'You are a thoughtful girl,' he said, 'and I do need these.' He quickly wrapped the scarf around him, thinking, What I don't need is you here to worry about and distract me.'

As if reading his mind, she said, 'I won't get in the way, Ernest, I promise.'

Best pulled on the gloves. The extra warmth was certainly welcome. 'You came all this way alone?' he said, grasping her hands. She was a dear girl.

'I'm not a child,' she said, suddenly defensive, then she put her head on one side and smiled her most fetching smile, 'besides I thought it might be fun.'

'It will be, I'm sure.' He patted her hand distractedly, looking around as he did to see that no one else was sneaking into the forbidden area.

A gasp from the crowd made his head swing rapidly around towards the balloons. The French balloon had begun to jerk and drag itself upright. The Eclipse started to follow suit.

'Back in the crowd, please, dearest,' he said, pushing her away without looking around. Both balloons were growing larger by the second. The ropes holding them tautened as the north-east wind began pulling at them, urging them to leave the earth now and fly with it. 'I'll see you later.'

He sensed that Mary Jane hadn't moved.

She was transfixed. 'Do as I tell you,' he yelled. 'Move away!'

Much more checking of ropes and ballast took place. A premature flight, without a crew, was the last thing they wanted.

As the time for lift-off drew near, the policemen kept exchanging anxious looks and scanning the crowd, alert to the danger of a sudden attack. Best's fingers dug into his palm. Please let this go all right, he whispered to himself. Please.

He knew they had done everything they could to make sure it did. Uniformed policemen had spent all night searching in and around the glass palace. All those people anywhere near the balloons had been checked and rechecked, and the official inspection teams had been extra thorough in their perusal of the craft.

But somehow Best still felt that if anything went wrong, it was his fault.

His fault because it was his reaction to what had happened all those years ago that had caused the problem. And his fault because he should have realized earlier who Quicksilver was.

Bigger and bigger the spheres became, jerking and pulling themselves ever upright.

Close up, they were certainly a breath-taking sight. So huge and awesome, swaying uncertainly in the wind as though warning that, soon, nothing would hold them back.

The crew were evidently of the same mind, for all at once they were aboard, some ropes were being slackened, others straining as the crafts were held above ground while ballast was ejected.

Then, in a flurry of flag-waving and enthusiastic shouts, the French balloon was up and away. A minute later, Eclipse rose gracefully and followed her.

How quickly they grew smaller as they began drifting southwards – without, Best noted with relief, either exploding or catcing fire.

He unballed his fists, let out a long sigh and shivered, suddenly aware that his socks were soaking wet. He gazed with disgust at his greying sodden boots.

Snow! In October! What next!

Twenty-Nine

It was magical inside the Agricultural Hall that night. The full moon shone brightly through the glass roof, lighting up the red and silver baubles on the Christmas trees and the tinsel swags draped across the side-show curtains.

The huge, silent hall, which had seen everything from prize cattle shows to colourful military tattoos, was currently springing to life twice daily with the Grand Christmas Fête. This featured spangled acrobats; a lumbering, bejewelled elephant; Blondin, 'the hero of Niagara'; and a dramatic re-enactment of the Siege of Paris.

Old George, a 'chesty' nightwatchman with a gimpy leg earned in the Crimea, was taking Rutter and Best on a private tour of the Christmas show attractions as proudly as though they were all his own.

As they followed the wheezing fellow up the stairs to the first of the tiers which ranged around the edge of the hall, Best realized that Rutter was hanging back a little. He soon saw why. Also, why the man had changed his mind about coming into the Aggy rather than sloping off for a tipple; he was stealing from the toy and trinket stalls.

Every now and then Rutter's hand would shoot out, quick as a flash, and seize a bar of chocolate here, a small glass ornament there, or a toy animal from a tree, and stuff them into the pockets of the greatcoat he was carrying over his left arm.

Best was stunned. What should he do? Arrest another colleague? There had already been bad feeling enough about Armitage. Some thought he should have made him put the rings back and just reported it as a break-in.

Best was still an unproved rookie but Rutter was becoming well thought of in the division. Not only did it flatter them to have someone so posh in their ranks, but his incredible arrest rate was helping their crime figures to look better.

Afterwards, Best discovered that there had been suggestions that Rutter was not above planting goods on suspects then accusing them of theft. But he hadn't known that then and neither had his superiors. Right then, the general feeling was, if anyone can rid them of Slippery John Irons, Rutter could.

Slippery was N Division's most persistent and elusive of burglars. A thorn in their side who single-handedly kept their crime figures too high despite Rutter's efforts. Joke was, they knew who he was, but couldn't catch him at work.

Best glanced back. Rutter grinned at him, took a flask from his pocket, saluted him with it and took a long swig, staggering slightly as he did so. He was drunk as well! Oh God!

They weren't even supposed to be in there. What could he do to stop it? Should he just face the man up?

'Excuse me, sir,' said a frozen-looking constable who had been hanging about, guarding the Eclipse balloon. 'I was asked to give you this.'

He proffered a page torn from a sketch pad. Neatly written on it was the message: 'Meet me in the Assyrian Court. I'm learning and drawing! Mary Jane.'

Best glanced around him. Smith, his bodyguard, was deep in animated conversation with Mr Coxwell. Best shrugged. The lad had already given up his involvement with the balloon race. No point in robbing him of further fun.

He began squelching up the now slushy path towards the sturdy, cylindrical North Tower. The whimsical mandarin hats of the twin towers amused him, belying, as they did, the serious purpose of the structures –

that of storing and pumping out the vast quantity of water needed to feed the fountains, cascades and waterfalls, when they sprang to life.

The vulnerability of the towers to Quicksilver's machinations, had caused police some concern. Ruptured tanks could cause the grounds to be swamped and put the crowds in danger. A recent small breach had given them fair warning.

But a thorough search had revealed nothing untoward secreted there, and the two policemen posted on each entrance had kept away any unwanted visitors.

Not only that, the top of the North Tower was currently in the very capable hands of Sergeant Major Carthew of the Royal Engineers who, with his assistants, had been charged with making scientific observations on the ascent and flight path of the competing balloons.

The North transept doors turned out to be closed, so Best shook the dirty snow off his boots and trudged along the terrace towards the Central entrance. At least, the lee of the building provided some shelter from the still keen north wind.

Below, to his left, the sharp outlines of the statues and fountains in the Italian gardens were softened by snow. Indignant coots and mandarin ducks slipped about on the half-frozen lakes.

Occasionally, a shaft of weak sun would spotlight a church spire in one of the distant Kentish towns or villages below.

Best's heart felt surprisingly light. The balloon ascent had gone without incident, which was one major hurdle over. There was nothing he could do about any other possibility, apart from keeping his eyes open.

The crowds were depleted, due to yesterday's postponement, and those that had come were dispersing quite quickly now. This was no weather to hang about. Who knows, maybe yesterday's debacle and the weather had also thrown Quicksilver's plans into disarray?

But when he thought about Mary Jane, his mood darkened. Her arrival had set his thoughts once again on Helen. He was confused by his reawakened passion for her and felt unable to resist it. How did she really feel? Had she just pretended when she said she was pleased he was to be married?

There *was* still feeling there, he was certain. Maybe, he thought wildly, she would agree to marry him now? If it were so, how could he cause Mary Jane so much pain? She was already desperately trying to emulate Helen with this 'learning and drawing'!

But she was young, wasn't she? Young enough to recover, with plenty of time to find another love among her father's police colleagues. Best had merely been there when she had grown up and she had fixed her sights on him largely for that reason.

They were climbing the stairs to the Aggy's second tier when Rutter's swivelling eyes caught a movement in the floor above.

'It's that bloody Irons!' he shouted when the man flashed briefly into view. 'That bastard!' Rutter exclaimed, as despite being drunk, he took off in pursuit like one of Mr Pain's rockets. 'I'll teach him to come on my patch!'

Best, caught unawares and still agonizing over the dilemma in which his thieving colleague had placed him, was slower off the mark.

As he rounded the top of the iron stairway, he saw them. Rutter had caught up with the runtish thief who was teetering on the edge of the railings which edged that floor. His agility was one of the reasons for his success and why he was so hard to catch. Even rooftops were no hindrance to him. Rutter regarded the man's activities as a personal affront, a blow to his masculine pride and a block to his ambitions.

On this occasion, Irons had obviously tried to escape by shinning up the decorative ironwork on to the floors above. But Rutter, the fastest constable on the division, old Mercury, had been too quick for him this time. He had hold of the man's legs.

Best made his way down the deserted north nave of the Crystal Palace. To either side were the various fine art courts, the magnificent Egyptian Court, guarded over by pillars from the Temple at Karnak and a row of gigantic statues of Rameses II was followed by the Greek; modelled on the Parthenon this was awash with statues of half-draped ladies and athletic, nude gentlemen who recently – after complaints – had been made decent by the application of fig leaves.

In the Medieval Court chain-mailed knights jousted against a backdrop of Gothic windows and lancet arches while Good Queen Bess and Mary Queen of Scots faced it out in the Elizabethan arena.

It was getting quieter, he noticed. The only sounds were very distant voices and the occasional creaking from the structures around him.

There was no sign of Mary Jane among the massive human-headed bulls of the Assyrian Court. He called out her name but his voice echoed eerily in the chamber.

She *had* said Assyrian, hadn't she?

He scrambled in his pocket for her note. Yes, Assyrian. That was right. But, just a minute, this looked like Mary Jane's handwriting, but something about it looked forced, as if she had been told to write it by someone else. Why on earth hadn't he realized that before?

Irons tried to kick his left leg free from Rutter's vice-like grip. At last he succeeded, but in doing so his foot jerked back and smashed into the policeman's ribs.

Rutter let out a roar of fury, grabbed Irons' testicles and twisted them. He screamed in agony and lashed out again.

It was his death warrant.

Rutter let go of the thief's legs and gave him a hefty push.

Irons wobbled for a moment, grabbing desperately for Rutter's arm, which the policeman pulled back as he watched the man topple forwards, screaming in terror as he fell three floors into the arena below and Rutter spread his arms wide and proclaimed, 'O! What a fall was there, my countrymen!'

Suddenly aware of Best's presence he turned, grinned and said, 'You saw that. Resisted arrest, didn't he? Struggled – and over he went. Gone to a better place, wouldn't you say?'

Cold panic had already started to grip Best when he heard the shout from far above. 'Up here, Best. This is what you're looking for, isn't it?'

Rutter was standing on one of the decorative railings, in the Upper Gallery of Crystal Palace. In front of him he held a woman. His right arm was clasped tightly around her and his upper body leant forward so she was forced to look down. It was then that he saw it was Mary Jane.

'Come here an' tell your lady friend why you ruined my life,' he shouted. 'Why you had to go and rat on me!'

What was he to do now? He was a desperate rookie again. Only this time the stakes were terrible.

'You won't mind if I push her off, will you, just to even the score?' Rutter taunted.

Best rushed back towards the stairs and began climbing, throwing off his gloves, scarf and overcoat as he went. Trying to think. Trying to remain calm.

'If I see any of your colleagues, over she goes!'

Best reached the floor below Rutter, took a moment to get his breath back then looked up to see that evil, superior, grinning face.

'Tell you what,' Rutter wheedled. 'You come here and we'll do a deal. Her for you.'

Oh God, thought Best, please help me.

He was now on the same level as Rutter, on the Upper Gallery used by cleaners and workmen for maintenance. He looked along the balustrade to where the pair were perched unsteadily. Mary Jane's terrified eyes, pleaded desperately above Rutter's hand which was clasped tightly over her mouth.

This time he must act immediately. This time he must not wait for the tragedy to unfold. He grabbed the stanchion with shaking hands, pulled himself up and stood opposite his enemy.

'Right, Rutter,' he said in a firm voice. 'Let me have her.' He reached forward with his right hand, holding on to the iron pole behind him with his left.

Rutter smirked, his eyebrows raised superciliously. 'All right.' He began pushing Mary Jane towards Best. 'Here she is – fair exchange.'

'Don't, Ernest,' gasped Mary Jane. 'He wants to kill you!'

'I know,' he said. 'He always said he would.'

Rutter kept his hold on Mary Jane as he said, 'He told on me, the bastard! I'm sure he's sorry now though!'

Best's right hand closed over Mary Jane's and he began pulling her towards him. He had her. She was within inches of him when Rutter gave her a violent shove – towards the abyss.

For a second she wove to the left and right trying to regain her balance. Best hung on desperately but she could not recover. She looked at him, shook her head hopelessly, then wrenched her hand free and went over the edge, falling towards the flagstones far beneath.

Best howled his disbelief and anguish.

Rutter's eyes were wild.

'Gone to a better place, eh?' he screamed. 'Thought I was only going to get you. But this is better – much better seeing you suffer first!'

Best lunged forward, seized the smirking Rutter by the throat, and with a strength born of fury, flung him out into the void.

It was only later that he realized what the man had screamed as he fell.

'You're as bad as me! You're as bad as me!'

'You *never* pushed 'im,' insisted Cheadle vehemently. 'I was there.'

'Yes, I did,' said Best wearily. He didn't care about anything any more.

'You made a grab for 'im, got 'old of his coat, he tried to pull away, and fell. It's obvious.'

'No,' said Best. 'I know what happened. In the end, I was as bad as him.'

'Don't be stupid.'

'I can't lie about it.'

'So you're going to let that bastard win!' yelled Cheadle. 'Then you *are* worse than 'im.'

'Yes,' said Best. 'I think I am.' All he could

see was Mary Jane, in her brown coat, lying spreadeagled in the aisle below.

'Anyways, you don't have to lie,' announced Cheadle. 'We 'ave another witness.' He pushed Smith forward. 'Tell 'im what you saw happen, lad.'

Smith would not meet Best's eyes as he muttered, 'They were grappling, up there, and suddenly Rutter's right foot slipped. He tried to save himself but he began to fall ... Inspector Best tried to pull him back. But couldn't.'

A long silence followed Smith's pronouncement, Cheadle glaring at Best determinedly, and Smith keeping his eyes on the ground.

'No, no, John George,' Best said quietly, shaking his head and putting his hand out. 'When I taught you to fib, I didn't mean this. Not this.'

'I saw!' Smith yelled suddenly. 'He slipped!' Tears started into the young man's eyes and spilled down his cheeks. He wiped them away with the back of his hand, glared angrily at Best and shouted defiantly, 'Inspector Best put his hand out to try to save him – but it was too late!'

'He'd gone to a better place,' sighed Best.

'Right,' said Cheadle. 'That's what 'appened.'

He came right up to Best and fixed him in the eye. He was puce and shaking. 'You

302

wouldn't want to make a liar out of this young sergeant, would you, Inspector? To ruin 'is career!'

'No,' said Best eventually. He, too, was crying. 'I wouldn't want to make a liar out of that young sergeant.'